A HIGHLAND CHRISTMAS

PLUS BONUS MATERIAL

THE HIGHLANDS SERIES

SAMANTHA YOUNG

A Highland Christmas

Plus Bonus Material

A Highlands Series "Extras" Compilation
By Samantha Young
Copyright © 2024 Samantha Young

Edited by Jennifer Sommersby Young
Cover Design by Hang Le

A HIGHLAND CHRISTMAS

A Highlands Series Novella

PROLOGUE
HAYDYN

Five months ago

Ardnoch, Scottish Highlands

As soon as I opened the door and saw Kenna Smith standing on the other side of it, I immediately thought, *No way in hell*. It was bad enough interviewing people to replace Jean, a woman Michael adored and who'd made our lives easier for the last ten years, but there was no bloody way I was hiring an attractive young thing who'd get the whole village yammering.

A few years back, all anyone could talk about was the gorgeous American nanny Thane Adair had hired. The one who was thirteen years his junior and living on the property. I usually wasn't privy to local gossip, but the parents wouldn't shut up about it at school events, plus Thane's son Lewis was in my son Michael's class.

As it was, rumors turned out to be true that Thane was carrying on an affair with his nanny. He married her.

I would not put Michael in the position of having his father and new nanny gossiped about.

Kenna beamed up at me from the doorstep. "Dr. Barr?"

I felt a *flutter* in my belly at the sight of that gorgeous smile. Aye, this definitely wasn't happening. The next ten minutes would be a waste, but it would be unprofessional and illegal to shut the door in her face because she was gorgeous. "Kenna Smith?"

"That's me." Sunlight captured gold striations in her chestnut-brown eyes and I was struck dumb for a second. I'd never seen such beautiful eyes. Her smile dimmed. "Is ... oh, have you already filled the position?"

Tell her yes. I cleared my throat and stepped back to allow her entrance. "No, please come in."

Years ago, just before Michael started school, I'd decided I wanted to bring my son up in a village much like the one I'd grown up in near Aberdeen. After searching for plots of land to build a house, I found one on the outskirts of Ardnoch. It meant a two-hour round-trip commute to the university where I worked, but the village was everything I wanted for Michael. It had since turned into a bit of a tourist trap when local gentry and ex-Hollywood actor Lachlan Adair turned his family's estate into a members-only club for the Hollywood elite, but it was still a quaint and friendly place to raise a child.

Despite the fortune few knew about, I'd built a modest but luxurious three-bedroom home on the village outskirts. It had everything Michael and I needed.

"Your home is stunning," Kenna opined, eyes wide as she took in our open-plan living area. Kitchen, dining, and living space all in one with floor-to-ceiling glass windows to the front, overlooking our private driveway and the trees surrounding it. Sliding doors behind the kitchen led out to the back garden. It wasn't a huge space out there, but we were surrounded by picturesque woodland.

"I had an interior designer do everything," I admitted as I gestured for her to take a seat on the couch. "Tea, coffee?"

"A coffee, please. Milk, no sugar." She gazed around. "The designer did a great job. They really captured that modern midcentury look."

My mouth tugged up in amusement as I moved into the kitchen to make the attractive brunette a coffee. "You sound like you might know a thing or two about design."

"Oh no, not really. I just love home renovation shows." She chuckled and the husky, throaty sound caused heat to flare where it shouldn't.

Damn it.

Time to hurry this up. I quickly made her a coffee and sat across from her once she'd taken it from me. I was careful not to touch her in the exchange, though I noted her elegant long fingers and even longer legs as she crossed them. As she sipped the coffee, I saw a flicker of nervousness in her eyes that her cheerful friendliness was doing an imperfect job of hiding.

I knew from her application that Kenna was twenty-seven years old, had a qualification in childcare, and had been an early years' practitioner for five years. She'd moved on to working as a nanny but only had one previous employer for that on her résumé. I'd called her in for an interview, anyway, because I'd only had four people apply for the position. It wasn't easy to hire a nanny in rural Scotland.

"So," Kenna spoke before I could, "may I ask why you're looking for a nanny?"

Who was doing the interviewing here? I straightened in my armchair, greedily taking in her stunning face. She wore very little makeup, from what I could tell. A bit of mascara, maybe. Her olive skin was naturally tan, and she had a healthy flush to her cheeks that didn't look manufactured. I didn't think I had a type, but if I did, Kenna Smith was it.

Pointless, pointless interview. Still, I answered, "I hired Jean when Michael was a baby. She was a widowed nanny looking for a fresh start, so she moved out to Ardnoch to be with us. However ..." I smiled, happy for her, even though we'd miss the hell out of her. "She met someone on a dating app. Together, they've found a new lease on life. They want to travel."

Kenna grinned. "That's a good reason to lose her."

"Oh, very much so. And as she keeps reminding us, we're not really losing her."

"I bet not." She cocked her head. "So, is it just you and Michael?"

"Oh ... well, yes, since he was an infant. But without going into the details, Michael's mum has come back into his life." Deena's return had made me a nervous wreck this past year, but I'd do anything to make my son happy, and he wanted a relationship with his mother. "Anyway, I should ask you some questions," I remarked pointedly.

She flushed a delightful pink and some very bad thoughts sprang into my mind. "Of course."

I tapped my phone screen, looking at her résumé as an excuse not to look at her. "May I ask why you left your last employer and decided to move from Inverness to Ardnoch?"

Her hesitation made me look up. "We ... um ... I needed a change, and I have a cousin who lives in Ardnoch. She was looking for a new roommate."

There was something like unease in her eyes, suggesting that wasn't the whole truth. However, her last employer had given Kenna a good reference when I'd called her to confirm it, so I wouldn't push the subject.

"It's good that you already have accommodation because

this isn't a live-in position." *Not that you're getting the job.* After years of mistrusting women because of Deena, resulting in nothing but casual hookups, I'd finally decided it was time to stop letting one woman ruin my future. It would be nice to have someone to share a home with, for Michael to have a stepmum who cared. Unfortunately, there had only been two women who captured my interest in the last few years, and two other lucky bastards had beaten me to them. Since casual hookups no longer did it for me, it had been six months since I'd last had sex.

And I was not putting a long-legged brunette with eyes I could drown in, in temptation's range.

"Aye. My cousin lives in a flat on Castle Street and I'll stay with her until I can find my own place. And I have my car, so it's no problem for me to get here and take Michael to school and back." She gestured out the window. I'd been so busy looking at her, I hadn't even noticed the very nice Audi Q5 parked in my driveway. How did a twenty-seven-year-old nanny afford a fancy SUV? I turned back to her, and she shifted in her seat before taking a quick sip of coffee.

Fuck it. "Nice motor?"

She heard my nosy question in my tone and sighed. "It's a long story."

In other words, mind your own business. Difficult for me to do when I was supposed to put the care of my most precious possession in this woman's hands. The subject was moot, anyway. I'd already decided that I very much wanted to get to know Kenna Smith in the way a man gets to know a woman. I would not be hiring her, but I did want her phone number.

I'd allow some time to pass after our interview and then I could seek her out in Ardnoch to ask her for a date. I opened my mouth to bring the interview to a short end, but an engine sounded and cut me off.

I glanced sharply out the window to see Innes Williams parking behind Kenna's Audi. What the hell? The back passenger door of the old SUV flew open and Michael jumped out, hurrying toward our front door.

"Problem?" Kenna asked.

"My son's home early."

He was supposed to hang out with his best friend Grant Williams and his mum all day, so I could do these interviews.

"Dad!" Michael flew into the house as I stood from the armchair. "Mrs. Williams told me you're interviewing new nannies."

Bloody Innes. I cleared my throat. "I am. Michael—"

"Don't you think I should be here?" He crossed his arms over his chest and tilted his chin stubbornly. Even as he tried to stare me down, his gaze kept flicking to Kenna. He was lucky I found him adorable because he was also a pain in my arse. Deena and I had brought a smart kid into the world. Michael was precocious and too switched on for his age. Because it had just been him and me for so long, he believed everything should be decided as a team.

The only times I was reminded he was still a child were his excitement at Christmas and the way Deena had a way of turning his emotions upside down.

Before I could argue that no, I didn't think he should be here to interview his nanny, Kenna stood and held out her hand to him. "Hi, Michael, I'm Kenna."

Michael's arms dropped as he stared up at her as if she were an angel from heaven.

Fuuuuuck.

He shook her hand, suddenly beaming from ear to ear. "Do you like video games?"

"I do, and I'm really good at them. But I also like walking and football and going for bike rides."

His eyes widened in delight. "I like all those things too."

"No way." She grinned that enchanting smile. "So, what's your favorite video game right now? Let me guess ... *Fortnite*?"

"Of course."

"Cool. I like *Mizuki*."

Michael was practically bouncing on the balls of his feet. "You really play it? Do you want to play now?"

The front door opened before Kenna could reply, and Innes popped her head through. Her expression apologetic, she said, "I'm sorry. It slipped out and then he wouldn't stop pleading to come home."

"It's fine, Innes." It wasn't, but it wasn't her fault either. "I've got him."

"Okay. Have a nice ..." Her words trailed off when she caught sight of Kenna. "Day," she squeaked out and then shot me a look.

I'm pretty sure my expression begged her to help me.

Her lips pressed together like she was trying not to laugh. Then she waved at Kenna. "I'm Innes Williams. My son's best friends with Michael."

"I'm Kenna."

"My new nanny," Michael offered, making my stomach drop. "So you'll see her around. Come on." He grabbed Kenna's hand. "Let's play *Fortnite*."

Kenna looked at me.

I could feel Innes watching us.

My gaze dropped to Michael, whose eyes had grown round like a puppy dog, begging me not to disagree.

This ... this was why I didn't want him involved in the interviews. I would pick a friendly, warm-spirited older lady much like Jean. And Michael would pick the stunning twenty-something who knew who the characters in *Fortnite* were.

And because I was terrified of disappointing him the way Deena had his whole life, I knew at that moment I was sentencing myself to an indefinite period of blue balls.

ONE

KENNA

Present day

Christmas Eve, Ardnoch

Having lived in Scotland my whole life, I knew it was just the luck of the draw whether we got a white Christmas or not. For the first time, I wished for no snow.

So, of course, as I sat in Flora's, the most popular café in the village, I glanced up from my phone to see white flakes dropping from the sky.

Oh, vomit on cow turd. Eff my life.

"Mom, it's snowing!"

I turned toward the slightly accented voice to see Callie Harrow, a pretty blond in Michael's class, gaping excitedly out the window.

"Yeah, it is!" Her mom high-fived her, just as excited.

Our eyes met, and despite my worries, we shared a grin.

Sloane Harrow and her daughter were California transplants. We'd shared friendly hellos at the school gates and I'd bought delicious baked goods from the bakery Sloane owned across the street. She was engaged to a dauntingly massive fellow Scot, and I had it on authority from the gossiping mums at school that my boss, Haydyn, had shown an obvious interest in the gorgeous American before her fiancé won her over. I'd tried to ignore the flare of jealousy I felt at that information, just as I'd tried to ignore any romantic feelings I had for Haydyn.

It seemed he and Michael shared taste, however, because I was pretty certain Michael had a crush on Callie, who was a mini version of her mum. He teased her constantly and was highly competitive with her. More telling, however, was that before I came along, word had it he and Lewis Adair were pretty friendly. But the two boys had gotten into fights over Michael's teasing of Callie, who was Lewis's best friend.

I smelled jealousy on Michael a mile away, but he was too young to understand that's what he was feeling.

Time would only tell, and I'd keep my eye on the situation. It shocked me that ten-year-olds were talking about crushes and boyfriends and girlfriends, but when I thought back on it, I'd had a wee boyfriend in my last two years of primary school. In P7 we used to kiss behind "the huts," the mobile classrooms where they taught religious education. The memory made me snort inwardly.

"First snow?" I asked Sloane and Callie.

Sloane ruffled Callie's hair, the stunning diamond engagement ring on her finger winking in the light. "Second snow, but it's still pretty exciting for us." A look crossed Sloane's face that I didn't understand until she asked, "Will you be all right? If the snow gets heavy?"

Understanding dawned. The downside of living in a village was that everyone knew everyone's business.

When I moved to Ardnoch, I'd planned to get out of my cousin's flat and into my own home as soon as possible. The problem was that property was scarce in Ardnoch, and the only homes that had come up for sale were way too big. I could afford them, but I didn't need that much space. However, Una, my cousin, had proven impossible to live with. She didn't know how much money I'd inherited, but she knew I had money, and I'd noticed money going missing from my purse. Then she'd started asking for more money than I owed in rent and utilities. From there, she began raiding my closet and wearing my clothes without asking. It just got so weird and strained between us that I ended up securing a caravan on a caravan site out by the water. It was owned by a retired businessman. Gordon. He was lovely. And he'd given me a good deal on renting a caravan for as long as I needed it. I'd been in the caravan since late October, and it was bloody Baltic. Something I lied about every time Haydyn asked.

A bungalow had come up for sale just yesterday, though, and although it needed renovating, it was perfect for me. I'd viewed it, put in an offer right away, and it was accepted.

I told Sloane as much.

She frowned. "But that means you'll still be in the caravan over Christmas? While it snows?"

Not wanting to explain to her that I was spending Christmas alone and would be freezing if it kept snowing, I told her the same lie I'd told Haydyn. "I'm staying with family for Christmas."

She relaxed immediately.

I'd told Haydyn the same lie because things were strained between us too. I blamed Halloween, too much truth, too much bonding, and the electric chemistry that had zipped between me and my boss since he'd opened his door to me.

I knew he was a mistake as soon as I saw him. Dr. Haydyn Barr. A professor of civil engineering at the University of Highlands and Islands in Inverness. Handsome, clean-cut, chiseled jaw, almost pretty with his large dark, thickly lashed eyes and full mouth. Laughter lines around his eyes gave him some rugged weathering I found way too attractive. He was six feet tall, stylish, classy, intelligent, warm, a doting father—and ten years my senior.

The whole time he'd been interviewing me, I knew, despite how desperate I was for a new job and a new beginning, that I couldn't work for him. Not after what happened at my last job. However, Michael had blasted into the house, adorable and smart, and so desperate for female attention. I'd later learn that his mother abandoned him when he was a baby and hadn't reached out again until last year. Haydyn had taken the reconciliation with Deena slowly for Michael, but Michael wanted to get to know his mum. It was going well so far, though I knew it was still a worry for Haydyn.

When Deena asked to have Michael for Christmas, Haydyn had wanted to say no, but Michael pleaded to go and won. I was nervous about it too. Deena was married to a solicitor and they lived in Inverness. They had no children of their own, and the guy seemed nice enough, but I wasn't convinced he was interested in Michael.

Only time would tell.

So Michael was in Inverness for Christmas, and I'd told Haydyn I would be as well. That I had a friend back in the city who'd invited me to stay. That wasn't true. All my friends were back home in Aberdeen, and not one of them had thought to invite me for Christmas.

Even though they knew it would be my first alone.

Tears thickened my throat and I fought them back. "I better get on the road before the snow gets too heavy."

Sloane and Callie bid me goodbye and I waved to Flora, the owner, before I ducked out of the café. The cold white flakes weren't falling fast, but they were starting to stick.

Oh, bugger.

I burrowed into my scarf and hurried across the street to Morag's to pick up some last-minute groceries. I planned to watch a marathon of romantic comedies on my laptop and try very hard not to think about the fact that I was all alone.

Morag, a lovely middle-aged lady with pink-rinsed hair, owned the deli and grocery store. We chatted for a bit before I bid her a happy Christmas and opened the door to leave with my bag of premade meals I could heat up in my microwave, as well as wine, chocolates, and other snacks.

I hurried outside and smacked into a hard body.

"Oof." I staggered back, dropping my bag, as gloved hands grabbed my arms to steady me.

Blinking rapidly, my stomach flipped as I looked up into familiar dark brown eyes. Eyes that narrowed on me. "Kenna?"

"Haydyn," I squeaked out, looking and sounding like I was caught in a lie. Avoiding eye contact, I lowered to my haunches to pick up my fallen wares.

Unfortunately, so did Haydyn. He shoved my meals and the thankfully unbroken wine bottle into my bag and handed it to me.

"Thanks," I murmured.

"Shouldn't you be in Inverness?" he snapped with uncharacteristic belligerence.

"I-I'm just leaving," I lied.

Haydyn scowled. "And you're taking premade meals with you?"

"I—"

He held up a hand to cut me off. "I swear if you lie one more time, I'll ... I'll ..."

Amusement cut through my embarrassment as he failed adorably to find an appropriate punishment for me. Suddenly, the image of him taking me across his knee filled my mind and I squirmed, my cheeks flushing.

As if he read my mind, Haydyn's gaze turned low-lidded as it fell to my mouth.

And this was absolutely why he'd been avoiding me since Halloween. Every time we were alone, this sexual chemistry sparked between us, and it didn't take a lot to ignite it.

Seeming to shake himself, Haydyn straightened and cleared his throat. He wore a scarf knotted stylishly and tucked into his fitted black peacoat. The man dressed like he'd just walked off the pages of *GQ*, and it really did it for me. I'd never shown much interest in the way a guy dressed, but since meeting Haydyn, it was something I noted about the men I met.

"You lied. You're staying in that damn caravan over Christmas. Alone." His full mouth pressed into a disapproving hard line.

I shrugged. "You're staying alone."

"In a fully insulated home. Not a tin can off the coast of the North Sea."

I rolled my eyes. "Exaggeration."

"It's snowing!" he yelled and then seemed to remember we were in public.

"I'll be fine," I promised, not wanting his or anyone else's pity. "And it's temporary. My offer was accepted on a bungalow yesterday. Happy Christmas." I darted around him before he could stop me and practically ran toward my parked Audi.

However, I couldn't resist looking up the now snow-crested street. Haydyn stood under the dim glow of a street-light, staring in my direction. An ache of pure longing filled me as I remembered how he'd been on Halloween. How our night together was the first night since my life blew apart that I'd felt happy. Like I'd found home again.

Blanching at how wrong I'd been, I dove into my car. Yet as I made my way carefully through the falling snow toward the coast, the memories cascaded over me, anyway.

Two
Kenna

Three months ago

Halloween, Ardnoch

"That's Grant and his mum!" Michael yelled from the living room.

Hearing the childish panic in his voice, I darted around his room looking for those damn twin ninja daggers me and his dad had been reluctant to buy for his costume. Seeing the plastic blades peeking out from under his bed, I grabbed them. "Found them!"

Rushing out into the living room, I tried not to smile at how cute Michael looked as a dragon ninja. I'd spent hours on YouTube watching tutorials on how to paint scales onto his cheeks and forehead. Makeup littered the kitchen island, his dirty dinner plate on the counter, and he'd somehow managed to dump half the contents of his bedroom into the living area.

"Thanks!" Michael beamed up at me.

A few minutes later, Grant and Innes were in the house. Grant was also dressed as a dragon ninja, but his scales were blue while Michael's were green. He also didn't have face-painted scales, much to his chagrin.

"Thanks for outparenting me," Innes teased. "I'll never hear the end of this."

I chuckled as the boys stood together for the photos I insisted on taking. "You work full time, Innes. It's amazing what you accomplish."

"Thanks for saying that." She grinned at the boys as Michael slung an arm around Grant's shoulders and they posed with their plastic twin daggers. "The school is going to murder us if anything happens with those daggers."

"Or take them off them before they even get past the doors."

"Great," she muttered. "I'm looking forward to two very annoyed dragon ninjas if that happens."

Laughing, I took a few quick photos. Unfortunately, Haydyn was working late, so he'd asked me to make sure I got some snaps of Michael before he left for the school Halloween dance. Michael wouldn't be back tonight as it was a Friday and he'd be sleeping over at Grant's after the party.

We were making sure Michael had everything he needed for his sleepover when a car pulled into the drive. Ears perking, Michael rushed away from me to the window. His whole being lit up. "Dad's home!"

Warmth filled my chest as I watched Haydyn hurry out of his SUV. He must have gotten out of his meeting early so he wouldn't miss Michael. For the last few months, I'd watched Haydyn juggle a full schedule as a senior lecturer at the university, as a researcher, and as a freelance advisor on projects, not just around the UK but internationally. He did all that as a single parent. Yes, he hired a nanny because his life would be impossible otherwise, but I saw how hard he worked to make sure Michael never felt like he was missing out.

I'd found him physically attractive from the moment we met, but getting to know him had only intensified that attraction.

My stomach fluttered like a schoolgirl's as Haydyn burst through the door just as Michael flew at him. He laughed, embracing his son tightly before holding him back to study his costume. "Well, don't you look amazing!"

"I thought you were working." Michael grinned up at him.

Haydyn gently gripped his son's chin to tilt his face in the light. "I had to see my dragon ninja, didn't I? And look at you. You look awesome."

"Kenna did my scales. They're sick."

Haydyn sighed wearily at Michael's use of the word *sick* but grinned, nonetheless. "So they are."

"We better get going," Innes said, nudging Grant toward the door.

"I'll pick Michael up tomorrow." Haydyn stepped aside.

"I promised them breakfast at Flora's, so there's no rush."

"Okay, thanks, Innes."

"Bye, Kenna!" Michael waved at me and rushed out the door.

As soon as it closed on them, Haydyn turned and surveyed the room before his eyes fell on me.

There was that stupid fluttering again. I shrugged sheepishly. "I wasn't going to leave it like this for you. Let me tidy up."

"Don't worry about it."

"No, let me clear this all away." I gestured toward the hob as I began cleaning the island. "I left some pasta and garlic bread for you."

"You're an angel," he murmured as he strolled by. I tried

not to inhale the scent of his expensive cologne. A few seconds later, he said, "There's a ton here. Have you eaten?"

I glanced up from tidying. The answer was no and I was starving, but I'd been too busy feeding Michael and getting his costume ready. "Oh, I'll eat at home."

"There's plenty, and I can only imagine how rushed off your feet you've been today. I'm putting out two plates."

Ten minutes later, I was seated across from Haydyn at the small bistro table off the kitchen. It didn't take much to convince me to stay. Mostly because I wanted to be around Haydyn, but also because I was avoiding my cousin's apartment as much as possible. Things were not good there.

Since I was driving, I stuck with a glass of water with my meal while Haydyn poured himself a glass of wine.

"Long day?" I asked to distract myself from the sight of his fingers caressing the wineglass stem.

Haydyn swallowed a bite of pasta and met my gaze. "I'm close to finishing up a project, and it always feels a little manic toward the end. Plus, midterm papers."

I nodded. I'd kept Michael busy the past week because Haydyn had so much marking to do.

"You've been a lifesaver these past few months," he told me, eyes on his plate. "I was worried when Michael hired you, but it worked out."

I chuckled at his teasing, even though it was technically true that Michael offered me the job before Haydyn could. "I'm glad you're happy with his decision."

He shot me a smirk, but before he could say anything, his phone buzzed on the table. He reached for it and frowned at the screen. With a sigh, he turned it over and dug back into his pasta.

Finding myself more and more curious about my boss, I blurted out, "Everything okay? Someone bothering you?"

Since I'd started working for the Barrs almost three months ago, there had been no sign of Haydyn dating. If he was seeing someone, it was happening in the hours he spent in Inverness. Otherwise, he was totally dedicated to his son. Michael talked about his mum, Deena, after his visits with her, but I still didn't know the story there. Haydyn was a professor. However, that income didn't account for their luxurious home, car, and the designer clothes they both wore. Or the fact that Michael had everything a kid could ever need or want, including the fancy holidays Haydyn took them on every summer.

There was so much I didn't know about them, and I could only piece together the bits of information I'd gleaned over the last few months. Tonight was unusual for Haydyn because, although he was friendly with me, he tended to keep his distance as much as possible. Perhaps it was the sudden lowering of his guard—him inviting me to share dinner—that made me ask my slightly nosy question.

Haydyn looked up from his plate, his gaze searching mine. He looked handsome but tired. "It's a text from Deena asking to see Michael tomorrow. She asked to have him this Halloween, and I've already said no because she went behind my back last weekend and asked Michael to spend Christmas with her."

I knew Michael was spending Christmas with Deena because he'd been excitedly talking about it all week, but I hadn't known the decision was made without Haydyn. "Oh. That's not cool."

He pressed his lips together in a hard line before continuing, "Now I can't tell Michael no because he's excited, but I never planned for her to have him during such an important holiday. It's been less than a year since she came back into his life."

"She's getting pushy."

"Aye."

"You can tell me if this is none of my business, but how long was she out of Michael's life?"

Haydyn smirked unhappily. "His whole life, Kenna."

My lips parted in shock. "Are you kidding?"

"Nope." He took a sip of wine, and I could see it was to distract himself from the anger still brewing within. "I came home when Michael was six months old to find him alone, screaming the house down, sitting in his own filth. Deena had packed her things and left us. I could maybe get over her leaving us if she hadn't left my baby alone. She could have called a neighbor and asked them to stay with Michael until I got home, but she just left him. Anything could have happened."

At the fear in his eyes, I couldn't help but reach over to cover his hand with mine. "I'm so sorry."

"She had postpartum depression," he said. "I didn't know that until she wrote to me last Christmas, asking for forgiveness and to see Michael. There was a lot of back-and-forth between us for a few months before I asked Michael what he wanted to do."

"And he wanted to meet his mum." I lifted my hand off his and my palm still tingled from the touch.

"Aye." Haydyn dug into his pasta again.

"Did she explain where she'd been? Why it had taken so long?"

He nodded. "She'd started drinking to deal with her depression. She's been sober for two years."

"So she got sober, married a solicitor, and now she wants to be in Michael's life because *she's* ready to be in his life." Annoyance cut through me.

"Don't people deserve second chances?"

"Yes, but she also has to remember that it's just been you and Michael for ten years, and she can't waltz in and start making decisions without your consent."

Haydyn's gaze gleamed and that familiar spark of tension lit between us. The one we'd both been trying so hard to ignore. "I'm trying to play nice so she doesn't go after custody."

I didn't want to worry him, but he needed to be realistic. "Haydyn ... she's going to go after custody, eventually."

His expression tightened. "They always favor the mother."

"No, not true. They're not going to favor a mother who abandoned her child for ten years. At the most, she'll get visitation rights. So stop letting her get away with making decisions without your involvement. Christmas is done. But she can't get away with manipulating you and Michael like that. Michael is the one who'll end up hurt. The next time she pulls that crap, put your foot down. And if she threatens you with a custody battle, you remind her of the ten years she abandoned her child."

Haydyn sat back, watching me with an intense expression. "As much as I admire your fierce protection of us ... I sense a wee bit of reluctance to forgive."

"To forgive Deena? I've nothing to forgive. I'm just stating my opinion." My cheeks flushed at the thought of him finding me uncaring.

"No, I mean ..." He shrugged. "I don't know what I mean. I suppose ... What's your story, Kenna? I've told you some of mine. You've been working here for almost three months, and I have no idea what really brought you here."

My pulse raced a bit as I prepared to tell Haydyn the truth.

"Kenna?" His brow furrowed in concern.

I licked my lips nervously, fighting back the grief that still threatened to choke me. "My parents died on Boxing Day last year. They'd visited me for Christmas in Inverness and were driving home to Aberdeen. An oncoming car took a hairpin bend on the wrong side of the road. My parents died on impact."

Emotion brightened Haydyn's eyes and he whispered, "I'm so sorry, Kenna."

I knew Haydyn's mum was still alive and that they visited her in his home village near Aberdeen, and I also knew Haydyn's dad had died, so he had some understanding of my pain.

My smile almost collapsed into tears as I explained, "Between their life insurance, pensions, the sale of their house ... they left me a fair bit of money. That's why I have the nice car ..."

"And is that why you moved to Ardnoch? To be closer to family?"

The thought of my cousin acting like real family made me snort bitterly. "No. My cousin ... I don't think I'll be staying with Una much longer. She's not the easiest flat mate, and I'm pretty certain she's stealing money from me."

Haydyn sucked in a breath. "Why didn't you say anything?"

I shrugged. "I'm handling it, looking for somewhere to rent until something appropriate comes up for sale."

His brows drew together. "I don't understand, then ... why move here?"

My pulse raced harder, my cheeks flushing. "Because ... because the mum at my last job ... she and I got friendly. As you do when you're looking after someone's child. Her husband worked a lot, and she's a full-time teacher. And her daughter could be hard work sometimes. I tried to be as supportive as possible. Plus, she was so kind to me when my mum and dad passed. She gave me time off and was always checking in to see how I was doing."

"Okay ..."

"One night, about five months after my parents passed, she asked me to stay later for a girls' night. Her husband was away for work. After we watched movies and had pizza, she put her daughter to bed ... I made to leave ... and she kissed me and grew arms and legs when I tried to push her off. I had to shove her off me."

Haydyn's eyebrows rose.

I laughed, embarrassed. "Everyone always expects it to be the dad." I got up and began clearing our now empty plates. Haydyn stood, too, and followed me into the kitchen.

"So what happened?" he asked, taking over the rinsing of the plates.

"She apologized. And I told her I didn't feel that way about her but that we could just forget about it. I assumed it was just a slip-up because of the wine."

"It wasn't?"

I leaned against the kitchen counter as Haydyn cleaned up. "She tried at first ... to forget. But about a month later, she told me she had to let me go. She was too embarrassed and I think afraid I'd tell her husband. She offered to give me a good reference in exchange for leaving quietly."

Haydyn stopped loading the dishwasher and straightened. "Wow."

"Between that and the fact that I was fresh in my grief, I came here for a change of scenery."

"Has it helped?"

I lowered my gaze. "I'm feeling things here I didn't think I would ever have space to feel again after losing my parents." I looked away. "But it hasn't been all roses. Una's an awful roommate, and my friends back in Inverness seem to have forgotten I exist. I have some family back in Aberdeen. Una's mum, an uncle... but they were pretty awful after my parents died because they expected an inheritance. Everything got left to me, and I've had a few texts and calls asking for money."

"I'm sorry."

I looked at him. "Money really brings out the worst in some folks."

He nodded and settled against the counter beside me, our arms brushing as he crossed his over his chest. "Can I tell you something very few people know?"

"Of course. I'm a vault." Pleasure filled me at the thought that Haydyn trusted me so much.

He stared out of the main picture window that captured the trees surrounding the drive up to the house, and I recognized the grief in his eyes. "My parents divorced when I was fourteen, and my parents agreed that I'd live with my dad most of the time. I spent the summers with my mum and they alternated the holidays ... but it was mostly Dad and me. I adored him." He gave me a pained smile. "About a year after Michael was born, with Deena gone, we were living with my dad so he could help out with his grandson. And ... he won the Euromillions Lottery."

Shock froze me.

That was not what I'd expected him to say.

Haydyn glanced at me. "We didn't tell anyone except his financial advisors, bank, etc. We went on a fancy cruise together with Michael, and Dad bought the car of his dreams but kept it at a garage where no one knew him."

"Because he knew everyone would come out of the woodwork looking for money?"

"Exactly. So ..." Grief tightened his expression. "When he died suddenly the next year, and he'd left every penny to me ... I decided not to tell anyone."

I gaped at him, everything making sense. "Why are you telling me?"

"So you know you're not alone. Keep your inheritance to

yourself as much as possible, Kenna. Money does strange things to people, and you've already seen a glimmer of that. I mean, my mum doesn't know Dad won the Euromillions, but she knows he left me money. She makes snide wee comments now and then about how she spent years with him and got nothing ... even though I paid off her mortgage with my inheritance. Sometimes, for some people ... it's never enough."

I couldn't help myself. I reached out to curl my hand over his forearm. "I'm sorry, Haydyn. That you lost your dad too. He sounds like he was a good man." Tears spilled down my cheeks as I thought of my parents. My parents who I'd run every life decision past, who I still went on holidays with ... my parents had been my best friends and the two people in the world who made me a priority. Losing them was like losing a huge chunk of who I was. "I miss my mum and dad so much."

"Kenna." Haydyn turned and pulled me into his arms. His embrace was tight, comforting as I cried against his throat. "I've got you," he whispered hoarsely. "You're all right."

THREE
HAYDYN

Present day

The snow was sticking.

It coated the roofs of the quaint buildings on Castle Street, dusted car hoods, and sprinkled over fences and walls. Powdery whiteness lightly covered the cobblestones and pavements. The old-fashioned Victorian-style streetlights had come on, and it felt very much like we were just an hour's snowfall away from being in a Dickens novel.

Kenna drove away two minutes ago, and I was still staring after her. Yes, I'd been avoiding her, and yes, I should keep avoiding her …

I glanced up at the sky, at the snowfall that looked nowhere close to stopping.

"Did you see the news?"

The male voice brought my gaze down, and I locked eyes with an older male villager. I shook my head. "Not yet."

He pointed upward. "This came out of nowhere, but they say it's going to snow from now until tomorrow evening. We'll be lucky if we can get out our front doors by the time it stops."

Shit.

"Just getting some more supplies for the wife before we shelter in for Christmas. Thankfully, our daughter and grandkids arrived yesterday, or they'd never have made it up here."

I nodded at him as I strode toward my car. "Merry Christmas."

"To you too!" he called as I picked up my pace.

It was bad enough that this was my first Christmas without Michael in ten years and the house felt horribly lonely without him, but now I was about to do something I knew could break me.

Driving toward the caravan park where Kenna stayed, I cursed myself for going to her, even as I cursed myself for allowing her to stay in that damn caravan over the winter. Fear had kept my mouth shut. Fear of what I'd do if I let her close. And I had a right to worry about my actions after what happened on Halloween ...

THREE MONTHS EARLIER
Halloween

I'D ASKED KENNA TO STAY AND WATCH A MOVIE OR two with me. The thought of sending her home after her crying jag didn't sit right. Moreover, it didn't seem like her flat with her cousin Una was much of a home.

It truly was an innocent suggestion. We settled on the couch, snacks on the coffee table, and she'd told me a bit more about her parents and how close she'd been to them. I could fully empathize. The hardest thing I'd ever done was hold myself together for Michael after my dad died. All I'd wanted to do was fall apart. But I couldn't.

Soon Kenna's spirits seemed lifted. As if merely by talking about her parents and letting it all out, a huge weight had eased from her. That made me feel good, and my guard lowered. We chose a comedy, and I loved the sound of Kenna's laugh. Anytime something funny happened, we both looked at each other as we chuckled to see if the other found it funny, happy to discover that we laughed at all the same parts and groaned at all the jokes we felt fell flat.

Afterward, reluctant to lose her, I suggested we watch another movie. It was getting late, but I intended to offer for Kenna to sleep in Michael's bed so she didn't have to drive home in the dark. Kenna agreed easily to another movie.

We didn't know what to watch, so we ended up picking a new psychological thriller that sounded good.

Unfortunately, it was an erotic thriller.

A very graphic erotic thriller.

I tried to ignore my reaction to the sex scenes and why my reactions were heightened by the beautiful, kind brunette at my side. But when I snuck a glance at her out of the corner of my eye and saw her breasts heaving with her shallow breaths, desire struck me hard.

Her fingers were curled on her knees, her cheeks rosy pink.

"Kenna," I half groaned, half whispered as the sexy moans and whimpers of the couple in the movie played in the background.

Kenna's gorgeous gaze flew to meet mine. Whatever she saw in my expression made her reach out with a trembling hand. She placed it on my thigh and slowly moved it up, caressing me. Blood thickened my cock and it strained to break free of my trousers. Her hand had almost reached my dick when I grabbed it tightly in mine.

All rational thought had fled south.

I tugged on her wrist, yanking her against me, heat flushing across my skin at the sound of her excited gasp. A noise I swallowed in my kiss as I slid my palm beneath her hair to grip her slender nape. My kiss was voracious, and she met it with equal ferocity.

The taste of her. Fuck, the taste of Kenna Smith was unbelievable. It was right.

Her fingers sank into my hair as her whole body melted into me, and I tugged her over so she straddled my lap.

Months of pent-up sexual tension, and this was the explosion.

My skin burned and my nerve endings sparked and I was desperate to be inside her. Kenna's fingers flexed in my hair as she moaned into my mouth. My arms tightened around her waist, drawing her closer. Her breasts crushed against me, the kiss changing from passionate to pure sex. It was suddenly biting and wet, our tongues tangling and licking and learning every inch of each other's mouths.

It wasn't enough.

I squeezed her perfect arse and pushed her down on my lap so my hard-on rubbed her directly between the legs, but there was too much fabric between us. She whimpered, rubbing harder, seeking the friction, riding me until our mouths parted in brief increments to catch our breaths.

With a growl of impatience, I tugged her thin sweater off and Kenna raised her arms, our movements hurried and frantic as I divested her of the top and then her lacy white bra. Her small, gorgeous tits bounced with the movement.

"So perfect," I murmured hoarsely, cupping and squeezing them gently. "So fucking perfect." I captured her right nipple with my hot mouth and she cried out in pleasure.

Lustful madness took control of me, and I pushed Kenna down onto the sofa. She watched with a fiery, low-lidded gaze as I whipped off my shirt and then unbuttoned her jeans. Her eyes lowered to my abs, and the way she licked her lips hungrily made me thankful for the many hours spent at the university gym. Yanking down her jeans and knickers, I threw them to the floor. The whole time I devoured the sight of her. Perfect olive skin. All slender curves and long fucking legs. Plump lips parted on excited pants. Eyes flared with arousal.

So beautiful. So beautiful I'd lost my mind.

I came down over her, our lips crashing together, her hard nipples brushing my naked chest, her thighs gripping my hips. I still wore my suit trousers and her kisses turned desperate as she reached for the button and zipper on them. She pushed them and boxer briefs down and slid her hand inside to grasp and tug my cock out.

"Fuck!" I groaned at the sensation of her tight grip. I was throbbing and hot and hard and I needed either her hand or pussy. Preferably her pussy.

"Jesus." I thrust into her palm as she pressed my mushroomed head against her clit. She released me to grip my waist, tilting her hips as I teased her with just the head. I kissed her hard, feeling her wet against my tip. Needing her tight heat, I slid my cock to her entrance and began to push inside.

She grasped my buttocks, fingers biting as she moaned, "Haydyn, yes, please, fuck me."

Something about her saying my name cut through my fog. I froze, staring down at her flushed face and impassioned expression.

Hours ago I'd held her in my arms while she cried, grieving for her parents.

Kenna was vulnerable.

My son's nanny.

And I was about to fuck her. Bare.

Shit.

Her eyes widened. "Haydyn?"

I scrambled off her, horrified by my selfishness. I yanked up my boxers and trousers and dove to pick up her jeans. "Kenna, we can't."

I didn't get a chance to explain why I'd stopped. Kenna had jumped off the couch, hauled on her knickers and jeans, red-faced and angry. She'd stormed out, ignoring my pleading calls of her name.

My skin burned from the memory of that night as I pulled my SUV into the caravan site. Driving slowly past the caravans, I stopped at the sight of Kenna's Audi. It sat beside a static home. It was at least in the back row, farther from the water and tucked in between two other caravans. But it looked like no one else was on site, and the snow was sticking here too.

The next time I saw Kenna after that Halloween, I tried to broach the subject of what happened between us, but she said she just wanted to forget about it. And I was afraid to lose her from our lives, so I didn't mention it again. It stung that she'd decided she didn't want me after all, even though I knew it was for the best, so I'd avoided her.

Shrugging off all the reasons I shouldn't be here, I concentrated on all the reasons I should. There was no way Kenna should be living in a caravan during a snowstorm and no way she should be alone on her first Christmas without her parents.

Slamming out of the car, I hurried toward the narrow steps and didn't even make it to the door before it opened. Kenna stood there, still wearing her coat and shoes. A frown marred her pretty brow.

"You followed me?" she huffed.

"Grab your things."

Her eyes grew adorably round. "Excuse me?"

Impatience rode me. "Grab your things and get in the car. There's no way in hell I'm letting you stay in this caravan during a snowstorm."

She raised an eyebrow. "*Letting* me?"

Four

Just because he'd been bossy and domineering, I gave Haydyn the silent treatment as we drove to his place. It was childish. The truth was, though, my emotions were already heightened because of the time of year, and I was frustrated that I actually did need to be "rescued" by my boss. Staying in the caravan was silly, and possibly dangerous, in a snowstorm, so when I saw his car pull up I'd already decided that if he asked me to stay at his, I would. No matter the consequences.

But he didn't ask. He demanded.

Instead of parking out on the driveway, Haydyn reversed his car into the garage he only used during inclement weather. As soon as he cut the engine, he turned to me. "I'm sorry."

I reluctantly looked at him.

His dark eyes filled with remorse and concern. "I'm sorry I made you feel like you had to lie to me about your plans. And I'm sorry for being a belligerent bastard about it. It bothers me that you were going to stay out there alone. It bothers me you're out there alone, period."

My heart beat fast. What did that mean? Obviously, he

cared about me. But was that it? Was that why he threw himself off me on Halloween, as if he was disgusted? I tried to find my voice. "It's temporary."

Haydyn nodded with a heavy sigh. "Let's get in the house."

The garage was attached, so we didn't need to trudge back out into the snow. Haydyn let us in through the side door and I followed him into the warmth of the house. "You can sleep in Michael's room."

His words reminded me that he was all alone today too. He'd apologized for his attitude, so I decided to forgive him and put it aside. "How are you doing? With Michael at his mum's for Christmas?"

Haydyn shrugged out of his coat and scarf. "Honestly, it only hit me when I woke up this morning and he wasn't here. On Christmas Eve, we have our traditions. In the morning, I make chocolate chip pancakes and we watch *Rise of the Guardians*. Then we venture into the village, grab hot chocolate from Flora's, walk around for a bit, and then come home, have homemade chicken burgers and fries, and watch a marathon of Christmas movies until bedtime. Then I wait until he's asleep to bring out his gifts hidden in the locked closet in my bedroom. It's always been exciting for me too."

His expression was unbearably sad as he took my coat and scarf to hang up. "It's depressing knowing I won't be doing that tonight for the first time in ten years."

Sympathy ached in my chest. "It's just one year," I promised him.

Haydyn scrubbed a hand down his face. "Is it, though? And even then, I suppose this gives me a taste of what it'll be like in a few years when he's too old for this stuff. He already told me this year that Santa isn't real."

"Oh, he told me that too." I strode toward the kitchen.

"And I could see the hopeful, pleading glint in his eyes practically begging me to tell him different."

"Really?"

I turned at the smile in Haydyn's voice. "Aye. Really."

"What did you tell him?" He watched me curiously as I pulled a pan out of the cupboard and set it on the hob.

"I didn't want to outright lie, so I just shrugged nonchalantly and said, 'I wonder how Santa would feel about you saying that?' and left it at that."

He chuckled. "Nicely maneuvered."

"My point is," I continued as I pulled a bar of chocolate and milk out of the fridge, "Michael is still a boy, and you still have plenty of time with him."

"Hmm." Haydyn leaned against the kitchen island, arms crossed, the position straining the fine knit of his cashmere sweater around his biceps. "What are you making?" I glanced back at the hob as I dropped the chopped-up chocolate into a pan and then poured in milk, cocoa, and light brown sugar.

"Homemade hot chocolate." I glanced over my shoulder. "I thought we could keep some of your traditions alive. And it's snowing, so hot chocolate is a must."

His gaze searched my face almost tenderly. "I'm glad you're here."

Skin hot, I turned back to the hob. I was so confused. Haydyn had attempted to talk to me about Halloween, but I didn't want him to say to my face that he wasn't interested because I wasn't sure I could take it. Usually, I wasn't so fragile, but with Mum and Dad on my mind, that big gaping hole in my heart, I couldn't handle emotions as well as I usually could. And the truth was, I'd fallen in love with my boss. I'd fallen in love with both him and Michael. For months I'd been trying to convince myself that I was just lonely and latching on to the first people who came along who seemed like family.

However, even desperation couldn't fabricate the chemistry I had with Haydyn. It just *was*. I'd never wanted anyone the way I wanted him. I'd lost all sense of everything else but him that night on his couch.

I thought his springing off me like he was horrified meant he didn't feel the same way and had just gotten turned on by the movie we were watching. But now and then, I find him staring at me with his heart in his eyes, and it confused me ... because ... he stared at me like he might feel the same way back.

Sighing inwardly, I stirred the mixture until it melted and then I whisked it. Haydyn reached into the cupboard and pulled two mugs down. "Whipped cream?" I asked him.

He retrieved the can of fresh whipped cream from the fridge while I poured the hot chocolate into the mugs. Our fingers brushed as I took the can from him, and tingles shot up my arm. I expertly topped the mugs with whipped cream and then shaved chocolate over the top.

Handing one to Haydyn, I smiled but couldn't quite meet his eyes. "Happy Christmas Eve."

"Happy Christmas Eve, Kenna."

I shivered at the way his voice rumbled around my name and hastily took a drink.

Haydyn followed suit, his eyes widening. "This is delicious."

"Thanks. It was my mum's recipe." Rounding him, I made my way over to the sofa and tucked myself into the corner, getting comfy. The Christmas tree I'd helped Michael and Haydyn decorate stood in the corner. Fairy lights glowed around the edges of the large picture window. Snow fell outside, weighing down the trees and covering the empty driveway. It was a winter wonderland. So peaceful.

I sensed Haydyn taking a seat on the couch a little farther down. We sat in perfect silence, watching the snowfall, and it was ... lovely. Comfortable and lovely. For a while, I forgot to be sad about Mum and Dad.

When I was finished with my hot chocolate, I turned to Haydyn and found him watching me. I raised a questioning eyebrow.

"Are you okay? I know it's the first anniversary of your parents' passing in a few days."

Pain cut through the loveliness. "Do you want the honest answer?"

"Of course."

"I don't think I'll ever be okay. I think some years it'll hurt worse than others ... but losing them will always be with me because when I lost them, I lost a piece of myself. But I think we can be not okay about one thing and still find happiness in another." I gestured to the snow outside. "Hot chocolate on a perfect snowy day ... it's not too shabby."

When I looked back at Haydyn, he stared at me in awe. "Your parents would be so proud of you, Kenna. And I'm ... I'm so grateful that someone like you is in Michael's life."

What about your life? I felt like asking. *Are you grateful for me too?* Yet, I didn't want to ruin the moment with a possible truth that might hurt.

"Let's watch a Christmas movie," I blurted out.

Haydyn gave me a soft smile that was far too sexy for my own good. "Sure. You pick. I'll grab some snacks. What do you want to drink? I have a bottle of Laurent Perrier I got from my Secret Santa at work."

Alcohol plus Haydyn. Hmm. Dangerous territory. Still, champagne was my Achilles' heel. "Ooh, someone splashed out for Secret Santa."

"We had a fifty-pound budget," he explained.

"And someone at that uni knows how you spend fifty quid."

He chuckled as he stood and took my empty mug. "A glass of champagne it is, then."

FIVE
KENNA

The champagne was a bad idea. Not because I got drunk. But because the bubbly alcohol loosened me up. And when I loosened up, I suddenly thought it was a very good idea to seek out the truth and to speak it.

We'd been having a lovely afternoon and evening, considering we were both missing Michael, and I missed my parents. There was no need for dinner because we'd been munching on snacks throughout the day. Though I'd been nursing each glass of champagne, I was now on my fourth because Haydyn preferred wine to champagne, so the entire bottle was mine.

It's a Wonderful Life played on the television, and I partly blamed the movie for making me philosophical. Truthfully, Jimmy Stewart made me question why I wasn't forcing a confrontation with Haydyn. If I had feelings for him, why was I sitting on them? So what if he didn't return them? If I didn't speak up, we would never be together. And what if we were meant to be? What if Haydyn and Michael were my future and I let them slip through my fingers because I couldn't be honest? All these questions seemed perfectly acceptable in my tipsy brain.

I waited until the movie finished because Haydyn was enjoying it.

"They don't make actors like Jimmy Stewart now," he observed as the film ended.

"Nor Katharine Hepburn. Or Lauren Bacall."

He grinned at me. "That was when movie stars were movie *stars*."

"Hmm," I agreed. *Just do it. Just say it.* I took a breath. "Why did you stop us on Halloween?"

Haydyn blinked rapidly, clearly taken aback by my question. "Uh ..."

I turned to face him fully, encouraged by Jimmy Stewart and too much champagne. "Well?"

His gaze seared into mine. "Because you were grieving. And I didn't want to take advantage."

My lips parted in shock. That was not what I'd expected. "You weren't taking advantage. I knew what I was doing. I'm a grown woman, not some girl just out of school."

Haydyn grimaced. "Grief ... it can skew our feelings and emotions."

"So you stopped because you thought you were taking advantage of me at a vulnerable time?"

"That ... and you're my son's nanny. He cares about you, and I don't want to jeopardize that just because you're attractive and I haven't gotten ..." He trailed off, blanching.

Oh.

My stomach dropped in horror.

"Because I'd be a convenient fuck," I muttered, looking away as hurt flared hot and blinding.

"Kenna, no," he denied. "I didn't mean that at all."

"No." I couldn't look at him but my tone was soft, accepting. "It's fine. I get it. You're being a good dad. Michael ... Michael should always come first. And I wouldn't want to jeopardize my job if I'm just a convenient fuck to you. That's smart. You were thinking rationally. Thank you."

"Kenna—"

"I need a shower." I stood abruptly. "Do you mind if I use Michael's bathroom? Yes? Okay." I strode out before he could stop me and practically dove into Michael's room.

Of course, it was only physical for Haydyn. Why would he want me for anything more? None of my friends and family seemed to think I was worth remembering, so obviously I lacked that quintessential something that made people care.

My fingers trembled as I stripped off my shirt and jeans. It was true, then. When my parents died, I lost the last two people on earth who really loved me.

The thought was terrifying. I blinked past the tears, suddenly wishing I could jump in my car and keep driving. I was lost. Staying in one place I was lost, so I might as well be lost on the move, right?

The door to Michael's bedroom suddenly flew open and my heart sped up even faster with surprise as Haydyn strode inside. His nostrils flared at the sight of me standing in nothing but my red lace bra and green knickers. I'd considered the combination festive and hadn't thought anyone else would see them.

His gaze dipped between my legs, and my clit pulsed in response.

"Haydyn?" I whispered.

His hot gaze drank in every inch of me.

"If I was just looking for a convenient fuck, I'd go out and find a woman. You were never just a convenient fuck." Whatever he saw on my face made his eyes glimmer with tenderness. "This whole time, I've been worried what people would think if you and I got together. The other parents, the villagers. If it would subject Michael to gossip. But Thane Adair's children seem perfectly happy, don't they?"

Knowing he referred to Lewis Adair's father who married his nanny, I nodded, heart in my throat with hope I was scared to embrace.

"Why shouldn't we have what we want? We're grown-ups. And .... and I hate the idea that you think all I see when I look at you is an attractive woman. Every time I'm with you, nothing feels more real than our connection. It's not just physical attraction, Kenna. Though I've never wanted anyone as much as I want you. The last few months have been absolute torture." He gestured ruefully to his crotch.

Blood rushed in my ears at his declaration, my gaze falling to see his jeans straining with his erection. Oh my God. My skin flushed from head to toe, and my breasts suddenly felt heavy with need.

"In fact," Haydyn continued hoarsely, "I can't think straight. I feel like I'm coming out of my fucking skin ... and ..." He took a step toward me, hunger etched in his features. "That if I don't have you in every way a man can have a woman, I'll never be truly happy again."

Wow.

"Haydyn—"

His eyes flashed. "I want to hear you say my name as we make love."

Yes, please.

"Haydyn—"

"But first, I want to hear you say my name as we fuck."

I moaned. Because YES, PLEASE.

Then he rushed me. Our bodies collided seconds before our mouths did.

Haydyn's kiss was ravaging. It was a man's kiss. Dark, deep, and sexual.

His hand fisted in my hair as he held me, and I grasped on to him as he plundered my mouth. I whimpered against his tongue as his other hand gripped my arse to pull me into the erection straining the zipper of his jeans. The whimper turned to a moan, reverberating into his mouth. Haydyn ground his hips harder into me, squeezing my arse. I slid my hands under his sweater in answer, shivering at the delicious feel of his smooth, hot skin beneath my fingertips.

He groaned as I touched his nipples. The sound rumbled in my mouth as we kissed harder, messy, sexy, wild kisses I'd never experienced before in my life.

I needed him inside me.

Fumbling for the button on his jeans, I silently told him as much.

Then suddenly, I was in Haydyn's arms for a few seconds before finding myself on the bed, Haydyn covering my body as we tugged at each other's clothing. Well, he tugged at my underwear. Haydyn broke our kiss to unclip my bra with a deftness of touch that told me he was well experienced in unclipping bras. He took hold of it and ripped it away from me, throwing it over his shoulder. His fiery eyes devoured my naked breasts.

"One day—before Halloween—I came home early from work," he said as his hips undulated against me with a mind of their own. "You were helping Michael with a science experiment for school."

Bemused, I asked, "The potato osmosis lab?"

"Aye. For some reason it involved water and Michael was being a typical kid and splashing tap water everywhere. He drenched you. I could see your nipples, see your shape." He cupped me, squeezing my breast, and I pushed my hips into his undulations. Haydyn's hungry gaze moved to mine. "I had to hide in my room from you like a teenager because I was hard."

"Really?" I'd never have known. I remembered him being a wee bit brusque that afternoon but I hadn't known why.

He nodded. "That night was the first night of many I

showered with my hand wrapped around my dick, fantasizing about fucking you."

Wet slickened between my legs. "Haydyn."

He caressed me, plucking at my nipples as they tightened into hard points. "I lost interest in dating other women. I couldn't be with anyone else when all I could think about was you. And all the ways I wanted to make you mine."

"Do it," I begged, my mind a haze of lust. "Haydyn, please. I want you too. So badly."

His answer was a triumphant, plundering kiss.

I frantically pulled off his shirt, breaking the kiss to do it, wanting to explore his beautiful body ... but then he bent his head to my breasts, sucking a nipple deep into his mouth, and I forgot about everything but what he was doing to me.

I cried out, arching against him.

His long fingers curled around my underwear, and he tugged them down my thighs. They got caught around my ankles, and I kicked to get them off. My patience was obliterated. "I need you, Haydyn. I need you so much."

"Fuck," he murmured, his eyes wild with want. "I could only dream you felt the same way." He kissed me again, slow, languorous, torturing me with pleasure.

In answer, I fumbled for his zipper. As I slid my hand inside his boxers to feel his throbbing, hard heat, he slipped his hand between my legs, sliding his fingers into me. The wet he found there made him groan into my mouth. He tore his lips from mine, and my chest rose and fell in frenzied breaths as he stared into my eyes with a tenderness that filled me with certainty.

"You're beyond ready, sweetheart." His expression turned harsh with need, and he gently captured the hand I had wrapped around him and removed it. He pinned my hand to the bed.

Anticipation made me squirm beneath him. Haydyn

never broke eye contact as he shoved down his jeans and boxers just far enough to release himself.

Then he captured my other hand and held me down by the wrists. My panting filled the room, and I let my legs fall open wide as he nudged against me.

He pushed into me with a long, relieved groan.

My desire eased his way considerably, and that overwhelming fullness I'd been desperate for caused a pleasure pain to zing down my spine.

"More," I begged.

"Fuck, Kenna," he growled, his head bowing into my neck as he pumped into me.

I was mindless with want for him. My whole being, existence, became about Haydyn and the hot push and pull of him inside me. My hips rose to meet his hard thrusts, my cries and his groans filling the room.

He was surprisingly dominant, and it turned me the fuck on. I knew I was going to come quickly. The tension inside me tightened, tightened, tightened every time he pulled out and slammed back in.

"I'm close," I gasped because I'd never come with just penetration. "Haydyn, I'm going to come."

He released one of my hands to grab my thigh and pulled it up against his hip, changing the angle of his thrust. I reached for him blindly as the tension inside me shattered.

"Haydyn!" I cried out. Loudly. Disbelieving. Euphoric.

My orgasm rolled through me, my inner muscles rippling and squeezing around Haydyn. His hips pounded faster and then momentarily stilled before he cried out my name, his grip on my thigh bruising as his hips jerked with the swell and throb of his release.

As his climax shuddered through him, he let go of my thigh and slumped over me. Haydyn's warm, heavy weight surrounded me, and I slid my hands across his back.

Our labored breathing rasped in my ears.

My heart pounded.

Haydyn and I had finally given in to our attraction.

I'd just had the best sex of my life and it might even mean something much deeper than that.

But we'd also just had sex without a condom and Haydyn had come inside me.

Six

Kenna lay soft and warm in my arms. I woke up about half an hour ago, but she was still asleep.

After we'd first fallen over each other like horny teens, so clouded by lust we'd forgotten protection, I'd made sure to don some when I took Kenna into my room to make love to her. She made me laugh as I carried her out of Michael's room, anxious about throwing his bedcovers in the laundry all the while assuring me she thought she wasn't in the right place in her cycle and we should be okay.

Despite what I'd said to her, there was still a part of me worried that I was going to be the one who got my heart broken. That Kenna was still grieving and looking for a place to latch on to in her grief. That when she finally started to heal, she'd realize that and leave us.

But seeing her look so hurt thinking I only wanted her body, I couldn't let it stand. I couldn't bear to see her in pain.

And I wanted her so badly.

So I gave in.

Even as worries spun in my head about how this would

affect Michael, I couldn't deny how perfect she felt in my arms.

Brushing her hair off her neck, I trailed light kisses over her soft skin. She squirmed in her sleep, undulating her perfect arse against my cock.

Jesus, she was turning me into a teenage boy.

Reaching back for the nightstand, I grabbed protection and suited up. Then I set about waking Kenna with my fingers. Hot blood thickened my cock from semi to full mast in an instant at the feel of her warmth. I found her clit and circled it.

Kenna moaned, her eyes fluttering open. It took her a second to get her bearings. She glanced over her shoulder and her expression softened at the same time her lips parted on an excited gasp. "Haydyn?"

"Happy Christmas, sweetheart."

"Happy," she moaned, her fingers tightening around the pillow beneath her head. "C-Christmas. Ahhh, Haydyn."

Feeling her grow wet, I couldn't wait any longer. I gripped her hips and nudged her legs open. Finding her, I surged inside, squeezing my eyes closed at the perfection of her snug heat around my cock.

Our groans and cries filled the bedroom as I gently made love to her.

We came together. "Kenna," I groaned, shuddering against her as I trailed my mouth down her shoulder. "You're so perfect."

"That was certainly the perfect way to wake up." She giggled, and the sound filled me with a strange mix of happiness and desperation.

I didn't want to lose her.

Not yet.

Thus, I wasn't going to push the subject. We'd just enjoy

each other today. We'd help each other forget about the people we were missing.

Just as I returned from the bathroom after cleaning up, my phone rang on the bedside table. "It's Michael," I told Kenna as she sat up in bed.

She smiled but bit her lip shyly, making me want to kiss her. Instead, I grabbed my phone, eager to hear my son's voice.

"Happy Christmas, Michael," I answered.

"Dad! Happy Christmas!" He sounded excited and a pang of longing hit me. "I can't wait to come home and open my presents!"

I'd told him Santa would drop off his presents from me here at the house so I could still experience a bit of Christmas with him when Deena brought him home tomorrow.

"Did Santa bring you cool stuff at your mum's?"

"You can stop with the Santa stuff. Jim told me he's not real."

Anger tightened my throat and I choked out, "Jim told you Santa isn't real?"

I heard Kenna suck in a breath and looked at her. She glowered ferociously and mouthed "Fucking asshole" and I think I fell just a wee bit more in love with her.

"I'm ten, Dad, nearly eleven. I kind of already knew."

"Well, Santa doesn't visit people who don't believe in him, so that's probably why Jim thinks he doesn't exist."

"Dad." Michael laughed. "You don't have to pretend. Okay?"

I wanted to fucking kill Jim. It was bad enough Michael was growing up so fast ... did we as adults have to force them out of childhood? When I was a kid, there was nothing more magical than believing in Santa. Yes, it was heartbreaking when I discovered he wasn't real, but I wouldn't trade it for how bloody magical those eleven years of my life were when I still believed in him.

Changing the subject, I asked him what they were up to. Michael chatted away about the new phone Deena had bought him and games for his games console. Then he got quiet and asked, "Can I stay at home for Christmas next year?"

My heart lurched. "Why? Are you okay?"

"Yeah, yeah, it's fine. I just ... I like our traditions better. And I thought maybe I could just stay with Mum one weekend a month instead of at Christmas."

I smiled as I sat down on the bed. "We'll figure something out. But if you want to spend your Christmases at home from now on, you can."

A soft palm pressed against my back and I turned to see Kenna smiling at me. She slid her hand around my shoulders as she moved to press a kiss on my nape. The move made her naked breasts press against my back and arousal rose in me again.

Terrible timing.

"Do you think it's okay if I call Kenna?" Michael suddenly asked.

I stiffened, and Kenna felt it. "Uh, of course you should call Kenna. I'm sure she'd love to hear from you."

Kenna pulled back, eyes wide. And then she was scrambling out of bed. If she wasn't so fucking gorgeous, it would've been funny to watch her hurry naked from the room, presumably to get dressed and find her phone.

"Okay, I'll call her next."

"You do that. I love you, son. I can't wait to see you tomorrow."

"Love you, Dad. Bye!"

Less than a minute after I hung up, I heard Kenna's phone blaring and then her sweet voice answering, "Happy Christmas, Michael!"

My heart beat a wee bit faster. Because I wanted her to say

that to my boy. I wanted to hear her say it to him every year. But could I trust that's what she wanted?

***

I put my worries aside for the day. Instead, I enjoyed Christmas with Kenna. She talked me out of calling Deena and giving her an earful for letting Jim tell our son Santa wasn't real. We made breakfast together, and I tried to shrug off my annoyance. Kenna was playful and flirty in the kitchen, so that helped take my mind off it.

After breakfast, we sat down by the tree and opened our gifts to each other. Kenna had left the presents under the tree before Michael had departed for his mum's and she'd, thankfully, forgotten to take the gifts we'd bought her home.

She'd clearly snuck a look at my toiletries because she gifted me a bottle of my favorite aftershave, as well as a bottle of my favorite (and too expensive wine). "You shouldn't have," I murmured against her lips. "Thank you."

Kenna kissed me long and deep. When she pulled back, she whispered, "Someone needs to spoil you."

It was on the tip of my tongue to beg her never to leave. I cleared my throat and handed her the gift from me. It was a designer cashmere scarf I thought would suit her coloring. She smoothed her hands over it and oohed and aahed, like I'd given her the world.

Then I handed her the gift from Michael.

Her lips parted as she unwrapped it to discover the blue box with Tiffany & Co. on the front. It was an extravagant gift and one I thought would look better coming from Michael. "Haydyn," she whispered, tears filling her eyes as she opened the box to reveal the black velvet interior. Nestled on the velvet was a delicate 18K rose-gold necklace with two interlocking circles accented with carved Roman numerals.

"The girl in the shop said the necklace is part of a collection about taking time into your own hands and treasuring what matters most. The circles reminded me of your parents too. I thought it—Michael thought it was something you could wear to remember them."

Tears spilled down Kenna's cheeks as she stared at me as if she might feel the same way about me. "This is all you, isn't it?"

I shrugged. "It's from us both."

"It's the most beautiful gift anyone has ever given me. Thank you." Her fingers trembled as she took the necklace out of the box. "Can you help me put it on?"

I nodded, taking the necklace. Kenna turned, swiping her hair out of the way, and I gently fixed it around her neck.

When she turned, her palm covered the circles. "You're the most thoughtful man I've ever known, Haydyn Barr."

My heart hammered in my chest. "You bring it out in me."

Kenna's answer was to throw her arms around me and kiss me like there was no tomorrow. So I lowered her to the floor and made love to her like I might never get the chance to again.

SEVEN
HAYDYN

The next day, knowing it was the anniversary of Kenna's parents' death, I was watchful and perhaps a wee bit too much of a hoverer.

We spent a wonderful Christmas Day together, one that could've only been better if Michael had been with us. However, at night, we played in my bed, and we could be as loud as we wanted, which was phenomenal.

My first thought on Boxing Day was of Kenna, however, and I was disconcerted to realize she wasn't in the bed beside me. She was already up and dressed and making breakfast for us. She assured me she was okay, but there was a deep sadness in her eyes that I wished like hell I could take away.

It was an awful feeling of powerlessness to know that I couldn't.

The snow stopped overnight, and in typical Scottish fashion, the temperature had risen to a point that it was already melting. I'd just suggested we go for a drive to get out of the house for a bit when my phone rang.

It was Deena.

She wanted me to collect Michael.

"I thought you were dropping him off," I said, irritated on multiple levels.

"I can't. Sorry."

I hung up and explained to Kenna. I felt shit for leaving her. "Why don't you come with me?"

"No." She shook her head. "I'm not in the mood to see Deena, sorry."

"No, of course. I understand."

"I ... I should leave. Michael won't understand why I'm here."

"No!" I said louder than I meant. Kenna raised an eyebrow. I smiled apologetically. "Please, stay. I'll tell Michael I invited you over for Boxing Day."

"Oh. Won't ... will that not confuse him?"

Studying her, I realized she was asking more than just that question. She was asking me what we were and where we went from here.

Did I trust Kenna to know what she wanted when she was still grieving her family?

When she was in my arms ... the way she looked at me ... I didn't want to doubt that. But I had more than myself to think of. "We'll, uh ... we'll talk about that after, yeah."

Her expression dimmed, and I hated that I had to leave her. I pressed a hard kiss to her mouth. "I'll be back soon."

Kenna nodded, but I saw insecurity flicker in her gaze.

Damn it.

I'd need to make a decision and make it soon. I wouldn't be one more person who hurt this woman. It was difficult when I had my son to think of.

MICHAEL RAN STRAIGHT INTO THE HOUSE, CALLING Kenna's name.

Hearing the crack in his shout, I closed my eyes in a tight press, curling my hands around the steering wheel. I had to get a handle on my anger. I couldn't let my son see it.

Two hours ago, he had his mum back in his life and he was sweet and forgiving and excited about it.

Now …

The conversation I'd had with Deena just a little over an hour ago played around and around in my mind.

"We need to talk," my ex had said as soon as I stepped into her townhome. It was in a nice area of Inverness and while the house was narrow, it had three floors and was luxuriously appointed.

"Where's Michael?" I was already agitated that I'd had to leave Kenna when Deena was supposed to be driving my son home to me, and now this.

"Upstairs. In here."

I followed Deena into an office. "What's going on? Did something happen to Michael?"

"No." She leaned against the desk, nibbling nervously on her lower lip. She wouldn't meet my eyes. "Jim got offered a new job, and we can't turn it down."

"Okay?" I frowned.

"It's in London."

Fear scored through me. If she thought for one second I'd agree to Michael living with her that far away … I imagined a horrible custody battle ahead and what that would do to my son. "Deena—"

"Look." She held up a hand, still not meeting my gaze. "Before you worry about me trying to take Michael with me, that's not happening."

Why did that make me feel even fucking worse? "So … you're just going to leave him?"

Her cheeks reddened, and she finally looked at me before glancing away in shame. "This is a big opportunity for Jim, and we've talked about it and we know we won't have time to give Michael the attention he needs."

I hated this woman. At that moment, I truly hated her. "So, to be clear, after begging to have Michael back in your life, you're walking right back out again?"

She pushed off the desk, tone pleading. "We'd love to have him at Christmas every other year."

"No."

Deena flinched like I'd hit her. "What do you mean no?"

Seething, I hissed, "You do not get to play with my son like he's a fucking toy. You're in or you're out. If you leave for London, you don't get to see Michael again. If, when he's eighteen, he decides he wants you back in his life, that's his choice. But right now, it's my choice to protect him from his selfish mother."

Tears glittered in her eyes. "I knew you wouldn't understand."

"Oh, I understand, Deena. I understand that you want Michael on your terms and that's not what parenting is. You are a terrible mother, and I will never let myself forget that again."

Her tears spilled over. "And if I said I'd fight for custody after all?"

I huffed, no longer afraid of that threat. "I might actually have some respect for you if you tried, but one, I have a feeling your husband doesn't want a child around full time. Two, I don't think you could handle sitting in a courtroom being reminded that you abandoned your child. And three, thanks to my father, I now have more money than God, and you can bet your selfish arse that I will use every fucking penny to keep you out of Michael's life."

Deena swiped at her tears, angry defensiveness burning in her gaze. "I would have thought some time with me was better than nothing."

She didn't get it. "Deena, you abandoned him when he was a baby and he gave you a second chance without even blinking. Because he is so desperate for his mum to love him. And now you're going to tell him that you're leaving him again and you only have time for him every other Christmas? Do you not realize how much that's going to hurt him? Or do you just not care?"

She flinched again. "I ... I don't want to hurt him, but ... I didn't realize Jim would be so against having a kid when I wrote you that email last year."

"And Jim is more important than Michael?"

Deena's answer was silence.

To make it worse, she refused to tell Michael herself, and I had to tell him while we were driving home. He called Deena because he didn't want to believe me, and she reluctantly confirmed that she was leaving for London. That they wouldn't see each other for a while.

Michael had sobbed on the phone, telling her he hated her before he hung up. Then he cried and raged about it being Jim's fault. That Jim didn't like him. I hated my son had felt that from the bastard. Grief thickened my throat, and I'd had to pull the car onto the side of the road to comfort him. He fought me, wanting to be angry at everyone, before he finally collapsed against me in tears.

My own tears had slipped free, and all the old hurt and rage I'd felt toward my ex resurfaced. Yet I was angry at myself, too, for letting her back into Michael's life to do this.

The rest of the car ride home I tried to talk to my son, but he wasn't up for conversation. I'd told him Kenna was at the house and as soon as we'd arrived, he rushed out to her for comfort.

Controlling my emotions, I got out and strode into the house. I heard murmuring from Michael's bedroom, so I followed the sound and stopped in the doorway.

Kenna laid on Michael's bed and he was snuggled into her side. She stroked his hair and whispered soothing words. Her eyes met mine, and I saw the flash of rage in them before they filled with sad concern.

"I'm okay," I mouthed.

"You'll never leave us, Kenna, will you?" Michael cried, sounding so much younger than his years. "You'll never leave us."

Was it wrong that I wanted her to say she wouldn't? That I wanted her bound to us.

She searched my face and whatever she saw there made her expression soften with awe. Then, "I'll stay as long as you want me to," she promised.

And I knew then I trusted her. If not with my heart, I trusted her with Michael's. She'd never make that promise if she had even the tiniest bit of doubt.

Relief and joy cut through my anger, and I sank against the doorframe. "That would be forever, then."

Kenna sucked in a breath. "Really?"

Michael burrowed deeper into her. "Really," he and I said in unison.

That was the magic of Kenna Smith. She could take a traumatizing, sad day and uplift it with just her presence, like the sun through clouds. Even on a day that was painful for her too.

What had we done to deserve someone like her? Whatever it was, I wasn't looking a gift horse in the mouth.

"Forever," I repeated.

Kenna smirked. "Forever is a long time."

I grinned, more than happy at the thought of coming home every day for the rest of my life to this woman. "It goes by fast when the company's exceptional."

EPILOGUE
KENNA

Four years later

"Mummy, can we get a cat?" Willow asked from the child's play desk that sat in the corner of the living room. I noted the cat she was drawing as she watched an animation with singing felines.

"Perhaps when you're older," I hedged. Haydyn had bad pet allergies, so it was doubtful, but I was in the middle of cooking dinner and I didn't want to deal with my precocious three-year-old having a meltdown.

"Ask Santa," she pushed.

"I did. He said maybe when you're older."

Willow narrowed her eyes in suspicion and I almost cursed us for giving birth to such an intelligent child.

Thankfully, the perfect distraction was riding his bike up the driveway. This year, Haydyn had finally allowed Michael to ride his bike back and forth to school. I'd been nervous about it, but we'd agreed to give him that independence. The winter months bothered me the most, so we'd agreed he couldn't ride his bike during the short winter days and I drove him to and from school.

The schools just finished for Christmas break yesterday, though, and I'd given Michael permission to ride into the village to see his friends, as long as he came home before it started to get dark.

He'd only left an hour ago, so I was surprised to see him so soon. "Look, there's your brother."

Joy flooded Willow's little face, and she threw herself away from her desk with all the exuberance of a puppy, her brown curls dancing around her chubby cheeks as she rushed across the room. My heart ached at the cute sight of her bouncing on the balls of her feet, her hands clasped as she waited for her big brother.

There was no one Willow adored more than Michael.

Worry flickered through me, however, at the sight of Michael jumping off his bike and throwing it into the grass by the side of the house. He marched up the drive, disappearing from sight, but not before I caught a glimpse of the thundercloud that marred his expression.

He burst through the front door.

"Mikey!" Willow rushed him.

"Not now, Wills," he snapped impatiently and practically ran through the house without looking at me.

His bedroom door slammed.

And his baby sister burst into wailing tears.

Switching off the hob to see to her, I'd barely rounded the island when I heard my stepson's footsteps. He hurried back into the living room and swooped Willow into his arms, expression filled with regret. "I'm sorry, Wills." She hugged her big brother tightly, needing his reassurance. "Just in a bad mood. Ignore me, eh. Shh, Wills. I'm sorry. Let me make it up to you. Do you want to watch *Rise of the Guardians*?"

Willow sniffled and lifted her head from his shoulder. She wiped a chubby hand over her runny nose. "Yes, please."

Michael had sprouted in the past three months and was only a few inches shy of six feet now. Willow looked tiny in his arms as he hugged her close and carried her over to the sofa.

Pride filled me. I didn't know what had happened to put him in a bad mood, but I knew what it was like to be a teenager. To have my hormones all over the place and feel like I had little control over my emotions. The fact that Michael prioritized his baby sister over his mood spoke volumes about the kind of man he was growing into.

Just like his father.

I let Michael reassure his sister, let them watch the movie together, and didn't push to know the details of his bad day. I'd wait until Willow was asleep.

Haydyn returned home in time for dinner, and Michael, though quiet, still conversed with us. My husband, ever the observant father, noticed, however, and I managed to murmur the story of Michael's stormy return home to him while we cleaned up the kitchen.

"I'll talk to him," Haydyn had assured.

Later, after I'd read Willow's favorite book to her two and a half times (she drifted off during the third reading), I wandered into the living room to find Haydyn on the sofa.

"I made you a cup of tea."

I thanked him, grabbing the mug before snuggling in beside him. He'd switched off the main lights and just left the Christmas tree and fairy lights on. It was cozy.

My engagement ring winked against my wedding band in the light as I lifted my mug to my mouth. "Did you talk to him?"

Haydyn nodded, a wry smile on his lips. "Lady problems."

"Oh." Of course. Michael had had "girlfriends" before, but he was fourteen now. Girlfriends were starting to mean something a wee bit more serious. "Did he go into detail?"

He nodded. "He met up with his friends today. Callie Ironside was there."

I think I knew what was coming, and my heart broke a little for Michael. "Did he finally ask her out?"

"Aye. And she told him that she liked him but she was into someone else."

"Let me guess: Lewis Adair."

"She wouldn't say, but that's Michael's guess too."

"He really likes her, doesn't he?" I sighed, wishing I could give the boy everything he wanted. After Deena walked out of his life again four Christmases ago, she phoned now and then, but Michael was still angry. Instead of persevering through his anger, showing him she cared enough to deal with it, Deena gave up. Michael hadn't heard from her since.

But my son had a naturally open heart and he called me *Mum* now and I was honored.

Haydyn had involved Michael in his proposal six weeks after we started dating. It seemed fast to everyone else, but we knew we were meant to be a family. And I kind of loved the fact that Haydyn proposed before I could tell him I was pregnant with Willow. I'd barely begun living in my new bungalow when we decided I'd just rent it out and move in with them.

A lot of people probably assumed Haydyn married me because I was pregnant, and I decided not to give a shit what anyone else thought. We loved each other, and that was all that mattered. I was six months pregnant when we got married in a private ceremony with just Michael as our witness.

It was perfection.

"As much as a teenage boy can like a girl, I suppose," Haydyn replied.

"You don't think teenagers can fall in love?"

He grinned at me. "I think it's a different kind of love. I think ... the right girl will come along for Michael when it's time. I had to wait thirty-seven years for mine, but I'd have waited thirty-seven more. And so will Michael. It's just ... everything feels bigger when you're a teen. Everything's so life or death. I wouldn't go through all that again if you paid me."

I was still glowing from his "I had to wait thirty-seven years for mine." Snuggling deeper into his side, I shrugged. "As lovely as that is, I don't want him to have to wait for anything. I want him to have what he wants. He's had a crush on Callie forever."

"Maybe she'll come around." Haydyn shrugged. "There's a bit of a legend going around, though, about the Adair family."

I'd heard of it. "That once you fall in love with an Adair, you're a goner forever?"

"That's the one."

"Well, I don't believe it. I think the Barr men can give the Adairs a run for their money."

He grinned down at me. "I guess we'll just need to wait and see." Then he kissed me. It heated quickly and Haydyn reached for my mug, putting it on the side table so he could pull me more thoroughly into his arms.

We were so busy making out like teenagers that we didn't hear Michael walk in.

"Oh, gross." His voice cut across the room. "Aren't you both too old to be doing that?"

Haydyn and I broke apart, and I shot our son an affronted look. "How dare you? What age do you think I am?"

He grinned, seeming much more like himself after his talk with his father. "Old."

"Thirty-one is not old."

Michael poured himself a glass of water. "I hate to tell you this, but it kind of is, Mum."

"Wait until you're thirty-one. I think you'll have a different opinion then."

"Aye, aye, that's ages away." He threw back the water. "Carry on, if it makes you feel young."

"Santa is taking back all your presents!" I called quietly after him.

I heard his soft chuckle before he disappeared, and I turned to Haydyn. "You're a good dad."

He raised an eyebrow. "What makes you say that?"

"Because he's better after you talked to him. I love you so much. You know that, right?"

His voice was gruff. "I love you too. More than I knew was possible."

"Thanks for letting Michael hire me all those years ago."

My husband grinned at the reminder. He'd since told me that he planned from the moment he opened the door that morning to absolutely *not* hire me because he was too attracted to me. "My son always was smarter than me. But don't tell *him* that."

Laughter fell from my lips, and Haydyn ducked his head to swallow the sound with his kiss.

After another delicious wee make-out, I rested my head on his shoulder and we gazed at the Christmas tree lights. My fingers caressed the necklace he and Michael gave me our first Christmas together, and I thought of my parents. The sadness I felt didn't hurt as much now. I knew wherever they were, they could see I was more than okay. That Haydyn, Michael, and Willow had given me family again. That I was just as loved by them as my parents had loved me.

Knowing they knew that gave me peace I hadn't realized I'd needed.

"Happy Christmas, Haydyn," I whispered.

He kissed the top of my head and murmured, "Happy Christmas, my love."

THE BODYGUARD

A Highlands Series Novella

ONE
CASSIDY

Ardnoch Castle & Estate, Scottish Highlands

Standing on the beach, feeling the icy sea breeze swirl around me, I knew this was exactly what I needed. The clouds were a heavy gunmetal overhead, but they hadn't begun to weep into the sea, despite every sign that they would. The water matched the clouds in color; the waves crashed to shore with a loud rush. Its rhythm soothed me as I wrapped my arms tight around my body.

The smooth sand stretched for miles before curving out toward the North Sea in a jut of earth. I could walk alone along it and no one would bother me. The illusion of freedom was powerful because with it came the knowledge that this beach, this estate, was heavily guarded and secured. The manager, Aria Hunter, had assured me the drone security perimeter around the castle and its mammoth estate was the best in the world.

I was safe without feeling like I was suffocating.

Eventually, the cold sparked a longing for hot cocoa. Turning on my heel, I trudged up the sand dunes and onto the path that led back to the castle. It wound past a small inland loch that I couldn't help but stop and snap a photo of. I then sent it to my mom to prove I was somewhere beautiful as well as secure. She lived in Massachusetts and constantly worried about me on any normal given day, let alone on one when I was thousands of miles away.

These days Mom had real reason to be concerned.

The thought made me shiver and I carried on toward the castle, suddenly longing for the company of people. Or at least the knowledge that they were right outside my door. The estate was a members-only club in the Scottish Highlands, owned by ex-Hollywood actor Lachlan Adair, and it had belonged to his family for generations. Now, for a hefty fee, it was home to TV and film industry professionals. Members could either choose to stay in the castle during their visit or in the luxury cabins dotted around the estate. Some people even owned homes here. Including Aria, who was married to the Scottish actor, North Hunter.

I'd opted to take a room at the castle for my month's vacation. There was no way I could hunker down in one of those cabins in the woods alone.

Not that I'd be alone, I reminded myself as I spotted Brock McIntosh waiting for me at the start of the pathway that led down to the beach. The castle loomed behind him as he stood, legs braced, hands clasped behind his back.

He stood like a soldier.

It had taken some convincing for him to let me walk to the beach alone, even though there was really no need for his presence here. According to my agent, Judd, Brock McIntosh was an ex-Royal Marine. He was born in Scotland but had been living in the US for the past five years, working as a bodyguard. Judd had hired him because Judd was more father than agent, and he was sick to his stomach with concern for me.

For the past nine months, I'd insisted I didn't need extra security, but I didn't argue when Judd hired Brock three months ago. He'd followed my every step since. And when I announced I was taking a break at the club I'd visited only once since becoming a member, Brock and Judd insisted Brock accompany me. My bodyguard knew the head of security on the estate, a man named Walker Ironside. This allowed him entry, even though Aria had insisted that I wouldn't need my own security. My agent and bodyguard disagreed.

So Brock was my ghost. Haunting my every step.

It was irritating on multiple levels.

I hated the sensation of my independence being stripped away.

I hated the reason.

And I hated it was the reason Brock had come into my life.

The Scotsman was just about the sexiest man I'd ever met, so it was beyond unfair that he was my employee, and, worse, he didn't seem to find me at all attractive. He'd given no sign in the last three months that he saw me as anything other than an assignment. Though he patiently listened to me prattle on about my life. Sometimes he even grunted in agreement or offered a one-word response to a question. Yet somehow, I was more comfortable around him than anyone. Ever.

I cocked my head, studying his stoic but rugged face. He meshed seamlessly with the security guards here in his well-fitted black suit and white shirt. He had a square jaw covered in sexy auburn stubble that matched his dark red hair. There were a few strands of silver in both his facial hair and the thick, short hair on his head, and it only made him more appealing. As did the faint lines around his piercing gray eyes. Broad shoulders, tapered waist, and long, long legs—the man had to be about six and a half feet. At five four, I was tiny next to him. Especially in the flat-heeled boots I wore today.

"Hey." I slowed on my approach.

He jerked his chin in acknowledgment and fell into step beside me as we walked down the gravel drive to the castle. You could still smell the sea air, even though the beach was a ten-minute walk from here. I loved New York, but I had to admit, the fresh air here was pretty awesome.

The castle was a rambling, castellated mansion, six stories tall and about two hundred years old. It had turrets, and a flag of the St. Andrew's Cross flew from one parapet. Columns supported a mini crenellated roof over an elaborate portico that housed the double iron doors of the castle's main entrance.

A sharp, icy wind blew up the driveway, whipping my hair back, and I sucked in a breath.

I felt Brock's gaze, but he didn't speak.

The butler appeared at the door and let us in. I thanked him and halted abruptly.

When I'd left this morning, the quiet, opulent great hall had been empty of activity.

Now it was abuzz.

People moved across the polished parquet flooring, carrying decorations and furniture. The hall décor was tradi-tional. A grand staircase descended before me, fitted with a red-and-gray tartan wool runner. It led to a landing where three floor-to-ceiling stained glass windows spilled light down it. Then it branched off at either side, twin staircases leading to the floor above to the members' guest rooms. It could be partially seen from the galleried balconies at either end of the reception hall. A fire burned in the huge hearth on the wall adjacent to the entrance and opposite the staircase. Dark wood panels covered the walls and ceiling. Tiffany lamps scattered throughout on tables gave the space a warm glow.

Opposite the fire sat two matching suede-and-fabric buttoned sofas with a coffee table in between. More light spilled into the hall from large openings that led to other rooms on this floor.

There was a man on an extremely tall, laddered platform, attaching strands of fairy lights to the ceiling. Cascades of mini pumpkin lanterns suspended from the ceiling here and there.

"Ms. Ward." Aria Hunter cut across the melee of busy workers, her tight skirt accentuating her lush figure. She smiled, and it was outrageously glamorous. The manager of the estate could be mistaken for one of the fancy-faced guests. "I'm glad I caught you. I meant to tell you yesterday when you checked in that we're hosting our first Halloween party at the estate. Or I should say, a celebration of Samhain. I realize you might not have time to put together a costume, so I wanted to provide you with this." She handed over a gold sparkly mask.

I stared at it, confused.

"It's a costume party, but it's also a masquerade ball," she explained. Aria was an American, but unsurprisingly, her accent wasn't out of place here. There were a ton of non-Scots at the club. "And in a nod to the traditional celebration of Samhain, we're hosting a bonfire outside and there will be fire dancers. It should be spectacular."

"Oh." I tentatively took the mask. It sounded spectacular. And a lot for someone who needed to feel like a hermit for now. "Thank you. I'm not sure I'll be attending."

"Well, it starts at eight o'clock and takes place right here. I hope you can make it." She gave me another kind smile and sashayed away. I cut a look at my bodyguard to see if he was checking her out, but Brock's gaze darted around the room, as if on constant high alert.

The realest emotion I'd ever witness from him was three nights ago when I'd returned to my house in LA after filming in New York for weeks. Brock had checked the house over first before letting me settle in. Until we permanently dealt with my stalker, Brock was full-time protection and he stayed in my guest suite.

So when I pulled back the duvet on my bed to discover a pile of my underwear covered in a what looked like dried semen, I screamed his name until I was hoarse.

Brock came running, half-dressed, gun in hand. There was a note on the bed among the mess. It was the first time I saw a slip in my bodyguard's mask. Fury etched into his features as he ushered me out. He made me stick by his side while he dressed and then we abandoned my house. Brock called the security company we'd hired to protect my LA home, and they checked video feed to see how my stalker broke in.

That night, I decided I needed to get away.

This had been going on for months, and I was exhausted.

Judd had hired Brock the night I returned to my New York apartment to find my living space covered in single red roses. This was after months of emails from a stalker whose love letters had started with longing and progressed into deranged delusions about our "relationship" until they got darker and more threatening. The kicker was, he believed I was a character I played, so he wasn't even obsessed with the real me. Did I mention the heads of the roses were cut off their stems?

Not exactly imaginative, but it freaked us all out enough to bring Brock on board.

For almost a year, I'd been afraid of my shadow.

I'd gone from a fiercely independent, award-winning actor who took no shit from anyone ... to being afraid to go anywhere alone.

He did that to me.

He stripped me of my peace.

His name was Freddy Watts. And there was little the police could do with no proof that he broke into my apartment. We got a restraining order, but anytime he broke it, he spent a night in jail and then he was out again.

The video feed from my LA house clearly showed him breaking and entering, so once the police caught him, we were hoping he'd do some prison time.

But the police had to catch him first.

And even then ... how long would he be in there? How long would I have peace of mind?

Two

BROCK

I followed Cassidy upstairs as she headed for her room. My room was a cabin on the estate. It gave me some much-needed space from the tempting bloody woman. We hadn't had space. We couldn't afford it until now. This exclusive estate in the Highlands with its first-rate security meant I could loosen my hold on her safety. I could probably loosen it much more than I was, but there had been a hollowness in Cassie's eyes since her home, her *bed,* was violated three nights ago. Worried, I wanted to keep a finger on her pulse.

As we strode into the luxurious suite with its incredible views of the North Sea, Cassidy turned to face me. She was quite possibly the most beautiful woman I'd ever met in my life, which was probably why a sick fuck had latched on and imagined himself in a relationship with her. Her striking green eyes had shone with light and humor when we met. Now they were tired and dimmed of the innate joy she'd exuded upon our first meeting.

If I ever got my hands on Freddy Watts, I'd kill him for that alone.

Cassidy gestured to the door. "You can head out. I'm staying in for the night."

"Are you sure?"

"I'm sure. I don't feel like attending a Halloween party."

"It might do you some good."

Her eyes flared at the suggestion. "And it might not."

Damn it. She needed to have a night of normalcy. Socialize. Remember who she was. But it wasn't my place to push her. "Right. Call me if you need me."

THE CASTLE THRUMMED WITH LIFE AS THE STAFF moved from room to room, preparing for the party. I cut through them all, making my way into the staff wing, toward the security team.

Walker Ironside, the head of security, was an acquaintance. We knew each other via a mutual friend, and I'd taken on jobs he'd found for me to guard other members of the estate. Both born and bred in Scotland, both ex-Royal Marines, we understood each other, although he'd done everything I'd done a few years before I had.

He was also one of the few men I'd met who was as big a bloke as I was. I knocked on his door and at his "Come in," I strode inside. This part of the castle was much more utilitarian and modern than the guest areas. Walker's office was a boring blank box with a small window to the outside. I'd be miserable if I had to sit in here.

"Brock." Walker relaxed back in his seat. "How's it going? Ms. Ward settling in?"

"As much as she can. I want Watts. I want to be the one to catch him, but I know she needs me here." I blurted this out, needing to say it to someone. And I knew Walker would get it.

He nodded grimly. "It's difficult when it becomes personal."

I tensed at the insinuation. "I just want her safe."

"Because it's become personal."

I'd been in private security for five years. During that time, I'd guarded other beautiful women. One even for an entire year.

None among them affected me like Cassidy Ward. I'd known who she was before the job, of course. Had thought little of her other than she was stunning, but uniquely so. She'd been the star of a hit streaming show about a genius female mathematician. It was set during the sixties, so it wasn't really my thing. But it had catapulted her to stardom. Posters of the show comprised just Cassie's face. That's all it needed to draw a person's gaze. She had wide-spaced, large eyes the color of which I'd never seen. They were violet. I thought they were contacts she'd worn on the show until I started guarding her and realized her eye color was natural. We were both redheads, but Cassie's hair was copper and vibrant. It was striking against her violet gaze. Amazingly, if you could get past her eyes, you'd land on her mouth, and that's where I always seemed to get stuck. Full lips with the most distinctive cupid's bow, red against her pale, freckled cheeks.

The woman looked like she belonged in a fucking fairy tale.

She was also ten years younger than me and a household name at only twenty-eight years old.

Now she was having to funnel some of her well-earned cash into paying me. To protect her from Freddy Watts, a man who believed he'd had a relationship with the character she'd played. Being famous swung your arse out there. It wasn't fair, it wasn't right, but it wasn't unexpected.

Though nothing could prepare a woman for finding a strange man's cum all over her underwear on her bed.

My hands clenched into fists as I remembered the fear and disgust on her face when I'd come running into her bedroom. Hearing her scream my name in terror was the worst thing I'd ever heard, and I'd been in war zones.

Because somehow in the three months I'd been guarding her, Cassidy Ward had crept under my skin. She never treated me like staff. Was always asking after my well-being. She chatted away to me about her days and divulged her vulnerabilities as if I were her best friend. Changed the radio station in the car every time she sensed I hated whatever song was blasting through it. Asked about my past and took it in stride when I offered her very little.

Smiled at me as if I could fix everything.

She hadn't smiled that beautiful, sweet smile of hers in three days.

Freddy Watts was going to pay for that too.

"Aye," I finally admitted out loud. "Aye, it's personal now."

I waited for his judgment. For him to tell me to walk away, let her hire someone else.

Instead, Walker exhaled heavily. "I've been there."

Surprised, I swallowed my natural instincts to clam up and asked gruffly, "How did you ... resist?"

He raised his left hand, flashing the gold wedding band on his finger. "I didn't."

I let out a low chuckle, even as my gut knotted at the thought of getting that serious with Cassie. "I'm not the settling-down type. Been there. Done that. Never again."

"I remember whistling that tune."

"I know myself." A serious relationship wasn't in the cards for me. "Anyway, any idea how to catch this fucker? For good?"

Walker's expression turned grim. "Nearly always, I've had

to wait for them to make their move and then take them down."

"Aye, that's what I'm afraid of."

"You'll stop him before he gets to her."

"I know I will." If Watts hurt Cassie, it would be because I was dead.

"You staying for the party?"

"I'm not a guest."

"Technically, you're the guest of a guest." He reached into his desk drawer and pulled out a set of keys. "You should stay. Enjoy yourself. Sometimes the best thing we can do is decompress in high-stress situations."

"I take it you're not staying." I gestured to the keys in his hand.

"Nah." He stood, grabbing his phone off the desk too. "I'm going home to help my wife babysit our granddaughter. And eat a shit ton of Halloween chocolate meant for the *guisers*." Guisers were what we Scots called trick-or-treaters.

"Granddaughter?" I raised an eyebrow. I knew Walker was older than me, but he didn't look anywhere close to being a grandfather.

"Daughter had a wee girl in February. Got married last week. Her and her husband are on their honeymoon. I've got a son, too, but he's only thirteen."

"Right."

Seeing the dubious expression on my face, Walker slapped me on the shoulder. "Was your age when it happened."

"What?"

"Your age. Met my wife. Sloane. She changed everything. My daughter, she's not mine by blood. Missed out on the first ten years. Luckily, didn't miss the rest. Never looked back."

Good for him.

"What I'm saying is ... don't count on 'been there, done that.' I've seen that look on your face. It was all over mine when I was protecting Sloane. A year later, she's got a ring on my finger and I adopted her daughter."

"Just because I care about Cassie doesn't mean I'm going *there*."

Walker nodded, amusement kicking up the corner of his mouth. "Cassie, is it?"

I glowered.

He chuckled, patted my shoulder again, and headed for the door. "I'll leave you to it. Try to take some time off. It might be Halloween, but there are no ghouls chasing after Ms. Ward tonight. She's safe in her room. And you look like you could use a drink." With that, he gave me a jerk of his chin and strode out of the office.

I rubbed a hand over my nape, feeling weirdly off-kilter.

THREE

CASSIDY

A massive bed sat in the middle of the luxurious suite and didn't even begin to take up space. The estate grounds were dark beyond the enormous bay window in the king-size room. Pale velvet curtains draped the window, and a light oak desk was situated beneath it.

A living area sat on a lowered level of the floor several steps down. There were more windows on the same side as the bay window, more darkness stretching for miles around outside them. The living area had a TV, but I wasn't in the mood to watch it.

The color palette was different in this room than most of the rest of the castle. More feminine. All the silvers and champagnes gave the room a much more tranquil feel than the heavy, traditional reds and golds found elsewhere. It was beautiful.

But it was suddenly closing in on me.

You know what? Screw this.

I was safe from Watts here. Why was I allowing him to turn me into a shuddering, scared shell of myself?

Sure, I wasn't a party animal. I'd never been a party

animal. But I was social and enjoyed being around people. As a lover of fashion, I adored any excuse to dress up.

Stomping angrily across the room to the old-fashioned armoire where the estate staff had unpacked my clothing, I rifled through it, hoping I hadn't imagined packing some evening wear.

There were hanging bags and, upon unzipping each one, I found cocktail dresses and an evening gown. One was a rose-gold Gatsby dress a designer sent me this summer. Reminiscent of the flapper, it was handcrafted with layers of rose-gold silk threads in rows of zigzag fringe. It had a plunging V neckline embroidered with contrasting gold lace and beads. I glanced back at the gold mask Aria presented me. It could work. A masked-up, roaring-twenties flapper girl could be a costume.

Feeling suddenly excited about this new distraction, I rummaged through my stuff, pulling together the vintage look. I showered first and then, after googling how to do it, I pinned my hair back after creating finger waves. Completing the style, I took a sparkly choker and fashioned it around my forehead, pinning it into my hair. Unfortunately, I didn't have strands of pearls, so I layered longer necklaces instead. It was a good thing I always overpacked, and I'd packed a lot, considering I planned to hide out here for a few weeks. I slipped on the sparkly gold Jimmy Choo peep-toe heels that weren't exactly era-appropriate T-bars, but the cross strap was close enough.

Tying the gold mask around my head, I stood in front of the mirror and let out a little laugh. I looked good! It reminded me of being a kid when Mom and I would cobble together a Halloween costume from stuff we had lying around because we couldn't afford the store-bought costumes.

Before I left the room, the thought crossed my mind that perhaps I should text Brock to let him know I was attending the party after all. Then I remembered I was safe here and maybe Brock just needed some time to relax too. To not constantly be on high alert.

Wandering down the hallway, I considered what Brock did in his free time. I'd thought about this a lot over the past three months. Anytime I tried to dig out personal information, he'd grow cool and distant. I knew how he took his coffee, that he was a weirdo like me who actually enjoyed healthy food, and treated his body like a temple. Moreover, I knew his workout routine because we'd taken to working out together. I knew he hated techno, jazz, and factory pop music. He loved anything with a rock edge, a little bit of country, and unconsciously hummed along to Florence + the Machine, Teddy Swims, and Lord Huron whenever I played them. He visibly frowned if a boy or girl band came on the radio and outright scowled if a song was all bass and digital beats.

Brock liked action movies and espionage shows. Some comedy. It depended. Hated anything with a hint of cheesy romance in it (like, he'd leave the room because he couldn't stand the internal cringing), and wasn't into anything set in the past. Correction: He said he wasn't, but I was pretty sure a certain character's death in *Downton Abbey* got him choked up. Though he'd never admit it.

This I knew.

His life before me, other than his professional credentials, I did not.

I wanted to know more—with more interest than was healthy.

I wanted to know what kind of women he liked. And I was pretty certain he was into women because I'd caught him ogling my ass a few times when we were working out. The look in his eyes was so hot, I honestly would have dropped my gym leggings in two point five seconds if he'd asked me to.

Though it was the only time he'd ever stared at me as if he realized I was female.

"Enough," I muttered to myself as I got into the elevator. For the past three months, I'd thought of nothing but Freddy Watts and Brock McIntosh. Tonight I was going to think only of myself.

The elevator dropped slowly and music hit me as soon as the doors opened. I strode out and through the archway into the crowded great hall. I grinned at the spectacle. Fake cobwebs, white and glittery, were strewn over every nook and cranny. Pumpkins, bats, broomsticks, wands, and stars suspended from the ceiling in playful artistry. Hidden projectors had created a dark, starry sky on the high ceiling, and through the music, sound effects created wicked cackles and spooky noises. Smoke machines pumping out mist meant I couldn't see past anyone's calves. Staff in black tailcoats and white gloves moved among the guests wearing black, sparkly masks. Nearly all the guests wore masks too. No one appeared to be dressed in a costume. Like me, they'd gone for the chic alternative of an "era" look.

I had no close friends staying at the estate. Sure, I had several acquaintances, friends even, who were members, but only one truly good friend. Penelope. She was one of the youngest female directors in the industry and directed me in *The Female Quotient*, the show that had made me famous. We'd connected instantly and had been friends ever since. But Pen was filming a new show back in LA.

I was pretty much on my own. Still, there was a possibility I knew some of these people behind the masks.

Grabbing a glass of champagne, I moved into the crowd and tried to shrug off the sense of unease riding my shoulders. Crowds had quickly become a place where someone like Freddy Watts could hide. Could jump out at me. I flinched at the image of him doing just that and stopped in the middle of the hall.

Then, as if on cue, loud, ominous, cackling male laughter cut through the sound system. The lighting dimmed and flared as a false crack of lightning flashed through the hall. Guests cried out in surprise and then a loud, sexy rendition of "I Put a Spell on You" played. My heart had lodged in my throat; perspiration gathered under my arms. Everyone burst into laughter, clapping and cheering at the creepy entertainment.

I'd never been one for enjoying a fright.

Even less so now.

Get it together.

You're safe.

A tingle scored down my spine, and I followed the sensation, glancing over my shoulder.

My breath caught as I locked eyes with a familiar man whose face was hidden behind a plain black mask.

Brock.

He stood against the wall near the archway I'd just come through. Still in his dark suit. Feet braced, hands behind his back. Alert. Watchful.

A quick look around the room told me there were two other security guards near the main entrance of the castle. Also in black suits and masks.

Was Brock working?

I glanced back at him, certain his attention was on me. But he didn't gesture or make a move, so I turned away. Now that I knew he was here, I was hyperaware of him.

Damn it.

Other than clearly liking my ass, I knew whatever Brock's type was that I wasn't it. Truthfully, until *The Female Quotient* came out, I didn't think I was many people's type. I'd always thought I was slightly odd-looking but grateful for my unique looks because they made me stand out in auditions. However, Penelope was vocal about how in love with my face she was. And even I could see that love on the show. She had the camera follow my every expression. Like a photographer obsessed with its subject.

Somehow, it made my uniqueness more appealing to a wider audience.

I got hit on more than ever and, of course, I even gained a stalker.

A tiny part of me wished I'd never done the show.

And I hated Freddy Watts for planting that thought because, until him, I'd considered the show one of my greatest achievements. I was so proud of what we'd created.

Brock admitted he'd never watched it.

I was strangely stung and euphoric at the same time.

If he liked me, it wasn't because of the show.

Problem was, he didn't like me.

I had a feeling women like Aria Hunter were more his type. Overtly beautiful in a more traditional sense, tall, dark, Mediterranean, with curves for days. Not five-foot-four redheads who looked more like an elven pixie than an Italian bombshell.

"Cassidy Ward."

I turned, mid sip of champagne, to find two men of average height standing before me. One was a brunette wearing a blue mask and the other a blond wearing a green mask. They both wore perfectly tailored suits, and I recognized them despite the "disguise."

"Johnny Hoskins and Ivan Welsh."

The hosts of a very famous comedy/celebrity talk show in the US. They grinned cockily. I had no idea they were members of Ardnoch. Their show had become popular five years ago and now they did a bunch of other TV shows together. Johnny and Ivan were famously arrogant, cheeky, and total players.

I'd been on their talk show multiple times, and they'd tried to get me to go out with them afterward, "to party,". I wasn't interested. But tonight, they were actually kind of perfect for a distraction.

We got to talking and moved into the dining room a while later because I was growing hungry, and the champagne was making my head fuzzy. I sensed Brock watching us leave, but I didn't let on that I was aware of him. Always aware of him. The guys flirted and joked with me as we ate and caught up with each other's lives. I didn't mention the stalker because it had been highly publicized and I didn't want to give Watts any more energy.

After a while, Johnny stood from the table. "Have you explored the castle?"

"A little."

"Have you been in the turret?"

"Which one?"

"The one in the guest area." He gestured to me. "C'mon, I'll show you."

"I'm not sleeping with you," I warned him, in case he thought this night was leading anywhere.

He grinned. "Of course not."

The turret turned out to be a charming reading nook, but Johnny was giving me this look behind his mask that I knew well. Somehow, he'd taken my warning earlier as a challenge. No longer inclined to be alone with him, I'd hurried from the turret. "Maybe it's time for me to go to bed."

"No." He followed me down the spiral staircase and out of the tower. Johnny grabbed my wrist, tugging on it. "The night is young. Look, there's an entire part of the castle that's off-limits to guests. It's one of the older sections. What night is better than Halloween to explore a spooky castle?"

I really wasn't in the mood to be spooked, but I was in love with history, which was why I'd jumped on the chance at membership to the exclusive estate here in the Scottish Highlands. Also, I didn't get creep vibes off Johnny and had heard no rumors that he was a dick. If I went back to my room, all I'd do was think of Watts again.

"Okay. But I'm still not sleeping with you."

"I get it, I get it. I promise. We're just exploring."

Following Johnny through the corridors, I quickly realized I was feeling a little discombobulated and hoped he knew his way back to the guest wing. Johnny held open a door that had Staff Only written on it. He gestured for me to walk ahead of him and the plush carpeting gave way to a flatter, older red carpet. The stone floor was visible along the edges of it. The walls weren't plastered here, and the exposed stone made it colder. I shivered as I strolled down the hall, glancing at the three closed doors we found. The corridor narrowed toward the end, an open archway leading me out onto a spiral, stone staircase that went up and down.

"What is this place?" I whispered.

When there was no answer, I turned. Dismay filled me to discover I was alone.

No sign of my companion.

"Johnny?"

Male laughter echoed ghoulishly down the stone stairwell.

A shiver of fear coursed through me. "Johnny, this isn't funny."

The sound of a door slamming downstairs made me jump.

"Johnny?"

Footsteps sounded. But not from below. From above. Downward, toward me. My heart rate accelerated and my legs shook as I took a step closer to the staircase and looked up through the gap. "Hullo?"

The footsteps stopped, and something like a growl filled

the stairwell. Suddenly, the footsteps started racing down toward me.

Call it Halloween creeping me out. Call it nine months of being terrorized by a stalker. Call it both. All rational and common sense fled and instinct kicked in. Blood whooshed in my ears as my heart raced, and I rushed toward the other end of the landing, almost tripping on my stupid heels as I ran downward. My mask was blocking my vision, so I ripped it off, abandoning it as I fled.

"Gonna get you, Cynthia," a deep male voice purred ominously, using the name of my character from *The Female Quotient*.

Like Freddy Watts. He called me Cynthia.

Tears of terror burned in my eyes, and I tripped, stumbling against the stone wall. I glanced back, seeing no one but hearing them, and lunged forward. Just as I reached the next landing, a tall figure stepped out of an arched doorway. Strong male hands grabbed me and I screamed, scrambling backward.

I tripped, going down hard on the stone stairs. Pain shot through my hip and I cried out.

Two masked faces appeared above me.

I screamed hysterically, trying to crawl back upstairs away from them.

"Cassidy, it's us!" A man laughed, pulling off his mask.

Ivan.

Johnny.

"It was a joke, babe."

I burst into tears, hard, wrenching sobs of relief and embarrassment.

"What the fuck?" a furious male voice clipped. Suddenly, Johnny and Ivan were physically shoved away from me, and Brock was there.

I cried harder.

His features were etched in pure fury, and yet his voice was gentle as he reached for me. "I've got you." I raised my arms to him, winding them around his neck as he lifted me into his arms with ease.

Burying my face in his neck, breathing in his cologne, I didn't look at Johnny and Ivan as Brock threatened, "You're lucky she needs me right now or I'd smear your fucking faces against that wall."

"It was a joke. A Halloween prank. We didn't know she was a head case."

Brock lurched toward them. "Oh, you are so going to wish you'd never met me by the time I'm done with you, boys." He brought me closer to his chest and strode away. I could feel his anger vibrating through him.

Yet I'd never felt safer.

Four

Brock

Cassie could probably hear my heart thudding against my chest as I carried her back toward the guest wing of the castle. She didn't seem to mind as she held tight, her face pressed to my neck as if hiding from the world. I gave her that. Because I needed to get a handle on my anger.

As soon as I'd seen her latch on to the pricks from that stupid US chat show, I was on high alert. My girl seemed a little desperate tonight. Needing an escape. A distraction. I didn't blame her for wanting that. I'd wanted her to have it, but not like this.

Johnny and Ivan were immature wee bawbags, and I should have known they'd choose someone to prank on Halloween.

Why her?

And then to laugh when they could see she was so distressed?

Everyone knew Cassie had a stalker. It had made global news.

Fuckers.

One of the security guards had come over to ask me a

question about private security and the next thing I knew, I'd lost track of Cassidy. I should have gotten to her sooner.

That was on me.

The rest was on them.

After I made sure Cassidy was okay, I'd find them and make them pay for what they did tonight.

As I neared Cassie's room, her palm smoothed over my nape and she brushed her mouth over the column of my throat. "You need to calm down," she whispered. "I can feel how furious you are."

A shiver rippled down my spine at her intimate touch. We reached her door and I lowered her to her feet, searching her face.

The fear was gone. Her color was back, though tears stained her cheeks and mascara ran at the corners of her eyes. I pulled the extra key card to her room out of my pocket and swiped it over the door. Then I pushed it open for her to enter.

"Please come in."

I couldn't deny her. Even though the intimate brush of her lips on my throat and her expression warned me I should walk away.

Following her in, I cleared my throat as I shut the door. "Are you okay?"

She unclipped her hair, throwing grips and the sparkly thing that had been around her forehead onto the dresser.

When she'd walked into the party earlier, I couldn't take my eyes off her. Only Cassie could show up to a Halloween costume party looking red-carpet worthy. She tugged at her hair and it spilled across her shoulders in exaggerated waves. "I just wanted a distraction. Now I feel like an idiot."

"You're not an idiot," I clipped out. "You're on edge and rightly so. Those two are immature fuckwads."

Her lips curled at my vehement curse.

Something in her expression put me on the defense.

"You care about me," she announced, as if it were a revelation.

Shit.

"Cassie—"

"You care about me," she insisted, taking a step toward me. Her chin tilted back to meet my eyes. I gravitated toward tall, curvy women because of my size. Didn't want to feel like I was crushing the woman I was with. Plus, I liked it rough. Wanted to move a woman into any position I desired without worrying I might hurt her.

But I couldn't remember wanting a woman the way I wanted this one. To feel her tight, wee pussy around my cock, her delicate tits in my big hands. The only lush thing about Cassie was her arse, and I'd imagined taking her on her knees, that arse in my palms, as I fucked her from behind too many times to count.

Sweat prickled across my body at the imagery.

When I didn't respond to her statement, Cassie offered, "You make me feel safe."

Something burned in my chest. "Good."

"Will you stay with me tonight? Here."

"No." I blurted out.

Her gorgeous violet eyes widened in surprise at my uncharacteristic denial. "No?"

"If I stay, we'll cross a line we shouldn't cross."

Cassie's breath hitched, and I felt that sound in my dick. "What line?"

"You know what line."

"Please stay with me."

I squeezed my eyes closed against the plea because I knew I was about to break and if I broke, it would fuck up everything.

Her hand touched my chest. "Please."

My eyes flew open as I gripped her wrist. Her breath

hitched again. "If I stay, I'm going to fuck you, and you don't need that right now."

Cassie's nostrils flared, fire flashing in her gaze. "I know what I need better than you do. Maybe I want you to fuck me."

"Maybe?" I growled.

"I do." Her fingers curled into my shirt. "I want you to fuck me, Brock. I just want to feel something that isn't fear or resentment or rage. I just want to feel ... good."

My cock hardened as my balls tightened. "You could go downstairs and pick someone more suitable to make you feel good."

The very thought made *me* want to shred the room apart.

"I could." She pressed against me, her breaths hastening as she felt my erection. "But I'm pretty sure you could make me come simply by stripping naked right now, so that's the level of distraction I'd like, and no one else will do."

Fuck.

Just like that, my self-control snapped.

FIVE
CASSIDY

One second, I watched as Brock fought against his desire. The next I saw him lose that fight. He gripped me under the arms, lifting me up as if I weighed nothing, and kissed me.

Brock's kiss was ravaging. It was a man's kiss. Dark, deep, and sexual. His stubble rasped against my skin as I wound my arms around his neck and my legs around his waist.

His hand fisted in my hair as he held me to him, and I kissed him hungrily in return. Brock groaned, pulling deeper at my mouth. It was as if he couldn't kiss me hard enough.

I whimpered against his tongue as his other hand gripped my ass to pull me into the hard-on straining the zipper of his suit trousers. The whimper turned to a moan, reverberating into his mouth. Brock ground his hips harder into me, slipping his hand under my dress to squeeze my ass. I needed him inside me. I wanted to be overwhelmed by him. To have all my senses captured by him. To feel and taste and smell and hear nothing but him, all around me, over me, in me.

"Fuck me, Brock," I broke the kiss to demand. "Fuck me and don't treat me like I'm glass. I'm not fragile."

Harsh intensity suffused his expression, and suddenly, we were across the room. He threw me on the bed and I bounced, excitement flipping deep in my stomach. I was wet already. So wet, just from his kiss.

He crawled over me, dwarfing me with his large, powerful body as his lips found mine again. I shoved at his jacket, wanting him naked. Brock broke the contact, sitting back, but only to take hold of my waist. He flipped me and I fell onto my hands and knees, startled by the ease with which he maneuvered me. A tug on the dress brought my focus back, and I shivered at the touch of his lips on the nape of my neck as he pulled the zipper down.

I sat up on my knees, shoving the sleeves down, helping Brock shimmy it off.

Twisting around, I turned for him so he could whip it down my legs. The thousand-dollar dress soared through the air behind us as Brock's hot eyes devoured me. I wasn't wearing a bra. His fiery gaze locked on my breasts. I didn't have big boobs, but I thought my B cups were perky and sweet.

Brock's gaze said he thought so too.

"Look at you." Brock's voice rasped with desire as he reached out to cup me. The touch of his large, calloused palms over my nipples made me moan. "Do you know how many times I've fantasized about taking your pretty tits in my mouth?"

Wet slickened between my legs. "Brock."

He plucked at my nipples, watching my face as I arched into his exploration. "Could you come with my mouth on these pretty nipples?"

"Yes!"

In answer, he bent his head to my breasts, sucking a nipple deep between his lips, and the tension inside of my womb tightened deliciously.

"Brock!"

His arms bound around my back, his fingers fisting in my hair. He tugged, pulling my head back roughly, forcing my breasts further into his mouth. The dominant action was like lightning on my clit. Months of tension, of wanting him, only to have him ... he laved at my nipple as his hands smoothed down my spine, and I felt my climax building.

Then he pushed his fingers beneath my underwear and slid them between my ass cheeks.

My orgasm shattered through me, and Brock released my nipple to watch me come.

"My god, woman," he murmured, awestruck.

I was barely cognizant of being laid on the bed, of him yanking my panties down my thighs. He stopped them just above my knees and as I reached to shove them farther, Brock batted my hand away.

His chest heaved as his gaze moved over me.

"Keep 'em there."

There went that deep, flipping sensation in my womb again. "Oh. Okay."

A slight smirk kicked up the corner of his mouth, and it was cocky and sexy as hell. This was really a whole other side to my bodyguard. He moved over me, slipping his hand between my thighs. His fingers pushed in and my hips arched off the bed. I tried to spread my legs, but my panties only stretched so far.

"Brock, please."

His thumb hit my clit and he started rubbing circles, hard, fast. My inner muscles were still trembling from the last orgasm, but Brock wasn't playing. This wasn't slow-burn torture. He wanted to set me off like a firecracker.

"Brock!" I cried his name as my belly trembled and my pussy clamped down around his invading fingers, the orgasm flushing through me.

As I shivered and shuddered against the bed, Brock sat back. His expression was so dark with want, he looked angry. He yanked at his suit jacket, shrugging out of it. Threw it on the floor. His shirt was next, unbuttoning it with speed and dexterity.

He revealed his golden, smooth skin, curving over hard, broad muscles that made my mouth water. I'd seen him half-naked before, but I hadn't allowed myself to really gaze at him.

"You're so beautiful," I whispered through my panting.

Brock's eyes squeezed closed for a second and then he was off the bed, but only to yank his wallet out of his pant's pocket and then drop his pants and underwear.

His cock was massive.

And swollen and red and pre-cum glistened at the tip as it strained upward with need.

My inner thighs trembled as I watched him take a condom out of his wallet and then roll it on.

Next to go were my panties.

Then Brock covered me with his big body and I spread my legs to let him settle between me. Hands pinning mine to the bed, he braced over me.

"Hard?" he asked.

Excitement shuddered through me. "I'll take whatever you want to give."

I let my legs fall open wide in anticipation as he nudged against me. Brock kissed me again. Wet and voracious. I moaned into his mouth.

He pushed inside. Hard.

My desire eased his way considerably, but he was large, thick, and that overwhelming fullness I'd been desperate for caused a pleasure pain to zing down my spine. I cried out, breaking the kiss.

"Fuck," he growled, his head bowing into my neck as he pumped into me.

If everything was out of control before, it turned wilder than I could have imagined. I'd never been so consumed. Everything was about the hot drive of him inside me. My hips rose to meet his hard thrusts, my cries and his groans filling the bedroom.

I couldn't touch him, could only take what he had to give, and it was so goddamn exciting, I knew I was going to come again. The tension inside me tightened, tightened, tightened every time he pulled out and slammed back in.

"I'm close," I gasped.

He abruptly pulled out, releasing my wrists to grab my hips. Like before, he whipped me over onto my hands and knees. I loved he didn't treat me like I was fragile. Wet soaked my inner thighs as a mini orgasm trembled through me. I moaned as he gruffly asked, "Steady?"

Yes, I was steady on my hands and knees. I nodded, unable to speak from breathing so hard.

Brock caressed my ass and then squeezed. "I have thought about fucking you like this more times than I care to admit."

I whimpered, pleased beyond belief that he'd wanted me too.

"Now you can have me," I choked out.

"Aye," he agreed, his grip on my hips suddenly bruising as I felt him nudge against me. "I can."

He thrust, the sound of flesh slapping against flesh filling the room as my back bowed against his drives. Brock swept my hair over my shoulder, one hand gripping my nape as he came over me. He squeezed my neck, possessive, dominant, while he held my hip steady with his other hand.

And then he *fucked* me.

My wrists almost buckled beneath the power of his drives.

"Your pussy's heaven. So tight. Soaked. Fuck," he grunted out, thrusting against my ass with his quick, hard strokes. "Come around me. Squeeze my cock, baby." Those dirty words were my undoing. Mr. Carefully Controlled, Vigilant Bodyguard Brock McIntosh was a dirty-talking, dominant bastard in bed. That wasn't a surprise.

How much I loved it was.

My orgasm rolled through me, my back arching, my inner muscles clamping hard around his cock. I cried out as it swept over me.

"Fuck!" Brock's hips pounded faster and then momentarily stilled before he cried out my name, his grip on my nape tightening, bruising, as his body jerked with the swell and throb of his release.

My strength gave out and I fell flat on the bed as he pulsed inside me. He released his hold on my neck and hip and braced, grinding his cock with a low, deep, sexy growl of relief.

Six

Brock

I could watch this woman sleep for hours and never tire of it.

That's when I knew I was in trouble.

Correction: I'd known for a while I was in deep shit.

Her copper-red waves spilled across the pillow, her lips parted slightly in sleep. The sight of her exaggerated cupid's bow provoked the urge to kiss her. She looked young in sleep. Too young. Ten years too young.

Cassidy had her whole life ahead of her. I'd heard her when she spoke of the kids she imagined in her future. I was past all that. Gave up dreams of fatherhood long ago because being a father meant being in a serious relationship, and I couldn't go through that fucking mess again.

And this woman ... I reached out to trail my finger over the curve of her cheek. She made me want things I knew I'd only regret in the end.

Last night ... I wanted to call it a mistake, but I couldn't. After Cassie had taken my fucking with an enthusiasm that blew my mind, I'd kissed and licked and sucked every inch of her perfect wee body until I was ready to take her again.

After another energetic round of sex, she'd fallen asleep in my arms and instead of getting out of her bed like I should have, I'd drifted off to sleep too.

Now it was time to leave.

The brutal ache in my chest made it one of the hardest things I'd ever had to do.

Cassie shifted in her slumber, and it was enough to move me to action.

Even as I dressed, I couldn't take my eyes off her. I took a mental snapshot of her lying replete and safe, naked, sexy, and soft beneath the sheets that fell around her waist.

Then I forced myself to walk out of the suite and not look back.

There was no room in my life for soft.

"YOU'RE POSITIVE SHE'S THE BEST?" I ASKED Walker, staring at the tablet screen in front of me.

It was five hours later. My mobile had a small list of missed calls and texts from Cassie. Every notification worsened that burn in my chest, but I was on a mission to make it right between us.

"It's Nicole or Roderick." Walker tapped the screen.

I'd enlisted him on a search for the best replacement I could find for myself. Cassie needed excellence at her back while Watts was still an issue.

"I'm leaning toward Nicole."

"I bet you are," Walker murmured, a slight bite to his tone.

I knew he thought I was making a mistake, but I knew better.

And so what if I didn't want another man in Cassie's space? I knew it would eventually happen, but I didn't need to be the one who set that shit up. Roderick was objectively a good-looking bloke, so he was out of the question.

"Nicole's excellent." Nicole Forster was once a special tactics officer in the Air Force. She was my age, had four years' experience in personal security, and was the Pan American champion in Brazilian jiujitsu two years ago. No family. No partner. Married to the job. She was perfect. "Can you make the call?" Nicole also worked for the security company Walker was once employed by when he'd been personal security to retired actor Brodan Adair.

"Aye." He took the tablet off me. "I'll let you know if she's available."

I sighed as Ironside marched out of the staff room without another word.

He didn't get it.

But this *was* for the best.

"WHERE HAVE YOU BEEN?" CASSIDY YELLED AT ME AS soon as she opened the suite door.

It was the next day. I'd successfully avoided her a full twenty-four hours. In that time, I'd spoken with Judd and we'd hired Nicole. And I'd spoken with Aria and Walker. They'd reviewed CCTV footage from last night, and after a quick discussion with the board of directors had booted Ivan and Johnny out of the club for what they'd done to Cassie. No fine. No warning. Just gone.

Those morons had faced the music. Now it was time for me to.

Seeing her was a hit to my self-control.

I strode past Cassidy with a blank expression, so I wouldn't give away my true feelings. There was no point confusing her with the mess inside my head.

"I've been making arrangements." I heard the door close behind me and turned to meet her gaze.

She flinched at whatever she saw in my expression. "What kind of arrangements?"

"For my replacement."

Cassie stared incredulously. "What do you mean? What are you talking about?"

"I can't do this." I gestured between us. "I don't want a relationship, and I can't guard you now that we've fucked. It has compromised my ability to guard you effectively."

"So you're quitting?"

The hollowness in her voice made that burn ignite. Fuck! "I slept with my boss. Aye. I'm quitting."

"Your boss." She looked like I'd slapped her. "That's all I am to you?"

No! It bloody well wasn't it.

But it was all she could be. "Ex-boss now."

My callousness might as well have been a punch to her gut. I saw it. The physical blow of my words. And I hated myself.

Unable to bear seeing the damage I'd inflicted, I strode toward the door. "Your new bodyguard is Nicole Forster. She's already on a flight. Walker will introduce you tomorrow."

"Wait ... Brock. Please."

I glanced back at her. Cassie's eyes filled with tears. I swallowed down my emotion and bit out, "She's the best. Trust me. I wouldn't leave you with anything less than the best. Goodbye, Cassie."

"Brock—"

But I'd already slammed the door closed between us.

Seven

Cassidy

Six months later

"**G**ood!" Nicole slapped my back, harder than I think she realized, and I smiled through a wince.

My new bodyguard was a badass, awesome motherfucker. Nicole was ex-Special Forces, a jiujitsu champion, and she was a woman's woman who fixed other girlies' crowns. Not only had she begun training me to defend myself, strengthening and helping me get fitter than I'd ever been in my life, she was supportive in other ways. When we were out and about and she was on duty, she was focused and tough and no one got near me.

But when we were just cruising in the car or hanging out on set or at home, Nicole could talk my ear off. She bolstered me when I was struggling with work, and she reminded me daily to keep in touch with the person who grounded me most. Mom.

Mom loved Nicole.

When she'd asked what happened to Brock and I burst into tears, Mom had insisted on coming to stay with me in New York for a few weeks. Both she and Nicole witnessed me try to piece together my broken heart, and it had bonded all three of us.

I wasn't sure I'd ever get over Brock, but I knew I deserved better than I got, so I had to remind myself he wasn't worth the heartache.

The police caught Watts and charged him with breaking and entering while I was still in Scotland. Brock had left Ardnoch without a word, and I'd remained there until I was notified that Watts was off the streets. A month later, he was convicted. Because he didn't steal anything (and even though he violated my bed), he only got a year.

I was now on month five of my freedom from him and I'd been making the most of it, filming an indie movie in New York.

The cast was young and vibrant, and they liked to party, so even though I wasn't a partier and not particularly in the mood, I threw myself into socializing with them. Nicole was my shadow. Nicole was concerned I was partying for all the wrong reasons. Like … hoping Brock saw the tabloid photos of me cozying up to my castmate, Ryan Whitman. Nothing happened between us other than a few sloppy kisses, but I wanted Brock to think I was over him. That I barely remembered him.

Now it was March. The film was wrapped, and I needed a break from partying. I wanted to enjoy my last month of freedom from worrying about my freaking stalker. Even though there were some memories there I'd rather forget, we returned to Ardnoch.

Nicole let me sleep off the jet lag before she had me in the estate gym working on my self-defense early the next morning.

"Okay." She smacked her hands together, giving me an

assessing look as I massaged my rib where I had a stitch. The woman had kept coming at me. I was pretty sure if I really got attacked, I'd be able to kick some serious ass after this. "You tired?"

I gestured dramatically to my body as sweat beaded down my forehead and I tried to catch my breath.

"Okay, good." Nicole was from Massachusetts, and her accent totally gave that away. "That means you'll be too exhausted to react when I tell you I found out this morning that your boy works here."

Confused, I scowled. "What boy?"

"*Boy* is probably the wrong term since that man is all man and that man is *fine*." Nicole wrinkled her nose. "Sorry, chickie. Your man is here. Brock. Turns out he's working here now as a security guard."

My stomach dropped. "No." I shook my head. "Uh-uh. He knows I pay a fortune for membership. He wouldn't dare take a job here knowing we'd run in to each other."

She grimaced. "Uh ... he dared."

***

SHOWERED, DRESSED IN A CUTE SWEATER AND JEANS, hair shiny and styled, I checked my reflection one more time before I ventured out of my room. I was on a mission to find Brock and tell him he was an asshole for taking this job.

Except my heart was pitter-pattering in my freaking chest as I marched down the castle corridor. Remembering the crushing sensation I'd experienced when I realized he wasn't coming back that morning he'd walked out of my suite, I squeezed my eyes shut for a second before I got on the elevator.

That man had put me through a roller coaster of emotions. I'd gone from euphoric after a night of the best sex of my entire life with the man I knew I was in love with, to anxious and disappointed the entire next day as he avoided me, to devastated when he walked out of my life like it was easy for him.

Taking a shuddering breath, I threw out thoughts of that broken woman who had cried on her mom's shoulder for weeks before pulling herself together in time to make a movie. Nicole had helped me become stronger.

I could face Brock.

And I could tell him to go find a job elsewhere!

He'd fucked me, dumped me, and then taken a job where I'd have to see him again. Uh, no! I allowed my anger to fuel me as I walked off the elevator and turned left toward the staff wing of the first floor.

"Uh, Ms. Ward, may I help?" a posh British male voice called.

I glanced over my shoulder to see the butler hurrying toward me. "Nope. Just need to talk to one of your security guys."

"Perhaps I can ask the person you need to come to you?"

"Nope. I'm good!" I picked up my pace before he could stop me, counting on the guy not wanting to be caught chasing after a club member.

"Oh!" A housekeeper came out of a door on my left and drew to an abrupt halt.

"Security guard room?" I asked, still moving.

"Second left and then first right," she answered, wide-eyed.

Following her directions, I marched into the security room. A man I didn't recognize stood up from where he sat at a bank of CCTV screens and two large computers.

"May I help you?" the large individual asked in a European accent.

"Brock McIntosh," I declared.

The guard raised an eyebrow. "Standing guard outside the gym."

"Thanks!"

I hurried away, pretty sure I heard him patching through to Brock. All the guards wore earpieces and were in constant contact with one another.

There was a part of me that expected Brock to abandon his post, so he didn't have to face me. The gym was housed in a building at the back of the main castle. Paving stones placed between a gravel driveway led from the castle exit to the gym and spa.

As I approached and the building came into sight, I saw Brock in the distance outside the door, legs braced, hands behind his back.

An overwhelming wave of longing and sadness hit me as I neared.

His expression was carefully blank.

How did he do that?

I was a professional actor, and I couldn't hide my emotions as easily as he did.

Then I saw it. I slowed to a stop as his gaze flickered over my face and the muscle twitched in his jaw. Giving him away. He wasn't totally unaffected by my sudden appearance.

"Cassie." Brock nodded.

"You work here?" I crossed my arms over my chest. "Here, Brock? Seriously?"

He raised an eyebrow. "Is that a problem?"

"Yeah. Because I got the impression last we spoke that you never wanted to see me again, and considering the way you bolted that made *me* never want to see *you* again, I'm pretty pissed you took a job where you knew you'd see me again."

He took so long to reply, I didn't think he was going to. "Walker offered me a job. I took it. End of."

"You took a job where you knew I'd have to see you."

"I took a job that was available and what I needed right now. You and I do not have to see each other during your visits. You're the one who sought me out right now. I'd intended to keep out of your way."

I flinched. "You're an asshole. I hate you and I hate being anywhere near you, so since I'm paying through the nose to be here, I'd really appreciate you moving on as soon as another job opens up elsewhere."

"Fine," he bit out.

"Fine." I whirled and marched away.

"Cassie ..."

I raised my middle finger at him without turning around and hurried back to the castle.

EIGHT

BROCK

You're an asshole. I hate you and I hate being anywhere near you.

Cassie's words played over and over in my mind, all the while clawing at my gut. The smart thing to do for both of us would be to let her hate me.

But after a day of walking around feeling like I'd been shot, I lost the battle to go to her. To make her understand. For six months, I'd buried myself here in Ardnoch. She haunted the place, and I couldn't get the memories of that night out of my head.

Because of my job, I was used to long bouts of celibacy. Before Cassie, I hadn't slept with a woman in three months because I'd been living with her and working a twenty-four-seven protection detail.

Six months wasn't the longest bout, but it was close. There was no reason for it. I could walk into the village and pick up a tourist or one of the few remaining single locals of appropriate age. I could go farther afield to Thurso or Inverness.

I didn't.

I'd tried.

But I wasn't over Cassidy Ward, and apparently, neither was my dick.

Time would heal the pining. I had to hope.

Yet when I saw her, even furious at me, it was like seeing a mirage of water after trekking for days through the desert.

Knowing that she hated me (and why wouldn't she?) was eating me up.

The next day, I strode into the small command center in the security wing of the castle. Aleksy was monitoring the system.

"Needing something?" he asked in broken English.

I searched the monitors where every public space in the castle and around the estate was displayed. "Looking for something," I murmured back.

There.

Cassie was taking a yoga class from the instructor, Eredine Adair. The bonny ex-dancer was the wife of the youngest Adair brother, and even though that family had more money than any one family needed, they all still worked at their respective jobs. According to Walker, Eredine had been the yoga, Pilates, and mindfulness instructor almost since the club opened. That surprised me since she didn't look old enough to have been here that long. I'd seen or met all the Adair siblings and their partners over the last six months. Happily married in a way that seemed abnormal. Loads of kids.

I wondered what it was like to have a big family like that. To be content to be with one another for the rest of their lives.

Eredine was adjusting Cassie's position. I tapped the screen over the live image. "How long has this class been in session?"

Aleksy frowned and glanced at the time on the screen. "Uh, they begin at thirty minutes after the two."

So nearly thirty minutes, then. "Thanks." I walked out

without another word.

Giving abrupt nods of acknowledgment to those I passed, I marched out of the staff exit and skirted around the side of the castle. The piper called out in greeting as he hefted his bagpipes into his arms. At three o'clock every day, the piper played his mournful instrument to signal the start of afternoon tea in the dining room. His song echoed around the estate.

You either liked the pipes or you didn't. For me, they made me nostalgic for home even though I was back in Scotland. I couldn't explain it, other than I was a bit of a traveling man and I didn't mind landing in new places and staying a while. But the cry of the bagpipes reminded me that wherever I was, I was a Scotsman and my motherland was in my blood. The only true home I'd ever known.

Following the gravel driveway toward the front of the castle that led to a path down to an inland loch, I came upon Eredine's yoga studio. It was housed in a modern building perched over the loch. The end facing the water was made entirely of glass.

I waited patiently outside it, inhaling the salt air as it drifted up from the sea I could hear in the distance, but was beyond my view.

About ten minutes later, the doors to the yoga studio opened and the handful of guests who filed out glanced curiously at me. Cassie was the last to leave.

She halted on the porch, glowering at me in disbelief.

Her yoga pants molded to legs that were curvier than I remembered. Curved with muscle. Biceps revealed by her tank top had a definition that wasn't there before. She'd been working out.

She got over her surprise and stomped past me.

My gaze trailed her. No amount of working out could get rid of that round wee arse of hers. Thank fuck.

"Wait." I marched after her, falling into step. "Cassie, we need to talk."

"The time to talk was six months ago," she replied coldly.

"You're right. It was. And I'm sorry for that."

She abruptly whirled on me. "What do you want?"

"To explain." The words were difficult to say. I wasn't a man prone to making himself vulnerable. "To explain myself because ... I cannot stand the idea of you hating me."

Cassie searched my face, and I saw a tiny flicker of curiosity before she closed her expression. However, she surprised me. "Fine. Talk."

"Fancy a walk down to the beach?"

She gestured for me to lead the way, and I followed the path that led down to the water. It took us past another inland loch before we reached the dunes. Sand covered my dress shoes and the hem of my suit trousers, but I didn't care. This was more important than keeping my uniform clean. We didn't say a word, though I was intensely aware of her as we strolled onto the empty sands.

There was no one else around, which was perfect because this was going to be hard for me.

"Well?" Cassie finally asked.

I glanced at her but had to look away because looking at her made me feel too much. "I ... I'm sorry for the way I ended our relationship. It was wrong and I should have handled it better."

"Thank you for saying that." Her tone was dull.

"I ... I was married once."

At her silence, I met her patient gaze. The waves rolled calmly toward my ankles, and I dared to touch her, leading her a little farther inland so we didn't soak our feet.

"You were married once?"

"Aye. Childhood sweethearts. Got together at fourteen. Married at twenty. Divorced at twenty-five."

"So, thirteen years ago?"

"Aye." It didn't seem that long ago. And yet it also seemed a lifetime ago.

"Her name was Fay. She was the prettiest lassie in school, and she made me laugh. A lot." My lips curled at the memories of Fay's antics. "I think of her as two different people. The lassie I loved as a kid. The person she became during our marriage was an entirely different woman." I swallowed hard. "Have you ever loved someone who changed so dramatically on you ... it fucked with your ability to trust anyone?"

"No," she replied softly. "I can't say I have. I've met people like that but never loved one."

"You begin to question everything. Your own memories and perception."

"What did she do?"

"The change began not long after we were married. We had little. She blamed me for that. I joined the marines at her encouragement. But almost as soon as I did, she started hating me for it. The worst part was that I finally felt like I was where I needed to be." I cleared my throat, keeping the emotion out of my voice. "I don't know who my dad was, but my mum died when I was four. There was no one to take me, and I ended up in the system. Foster home to foster home. I know now I clung to Fay because she felt like my first proper family."

"Brock ..." Cassie's soft voice around my name made me squeeze my eyes closed in pain for a second.

I opened them, staring out at the water as we strolled. "When I was home, Fay was always on my back. We fought all the time. But I'd claimed her as family and I kept hoping things would get better. About six months before the end, she was different. Softer. Funnier. Like my old Fay. We grew close again. And then she told me she was pregnant." That old familiar burn scored across my chest. "But we lost the baby."

Cassie gripped my arm. "Brock, I'm so sorry."

"The miscarriage was devastating. Fay was broken by it." I choked out. "I tried to get her to see someone, to get help. And that's when she told me that the baby wasn't even mine. That she was having an affair with our neighbor. Our married neighbor."

"Brock ..."

"Aye." I nodded grimly, still feeling the ghost of that betrayal. "I confronted him and it was all true. The only part that we'll never know for sure is if we lost our baby or if they lost theirs."

"I ... I don't even know what to say. I'm just so sorry."

I stopped, turning to face her. "I ... I can't attach myself to anyone again."

Her expression crumpled. "Brock, not everyone is Fay."

"I ..." I shook my head. "It's too hard. I'm sorry. But I need you to know that if it could be anyone, it would be you."

Tears shimmered in her beautiful violet eyes. "Somehow that hurts worse."

Fuck.

"I'm sorry." The apology came out in a gruff breath.

"I get it." Cassie stepped into my space, reaching up to touch my cheek. "I don't want to get it, and I wish I could somehow prove to you that you know me better than anyone. That I wouldn't change on you like that. That you can trust who I am."

"Cassie—"

"I know." She sniffled and retreated, dropping her hand. "I do understand. Thank you for finally telling me. I ... uh ... I think I need to be alone."

I clenched my hands into fists to stop myself from reaching for her. "Okay."

"Goodbye, Brock."

I didn't say it back.

I couldn't.

NINE

BROCK

Around eight o'clock that evening, I was just settling onto my couch to watch a documentary on the SAS when my doorbell rang. Considering I kept mostly to myself, I really didn't have that many people who would drop around the flat, let alone in the evening.

My place was small. A one-bed with a tiny kitchen and bathroom. But the living room was a decent size, and the bedroom was big enough for a king-size bed. The flat was above what used to be old public stables in the village, two streets over from Castle Street, the main avenue through Ardnoch.

I pushed up off the couch, pausing the doc, and crossed the living room. A peek through the peephole had my head rearing back.

Cassie.

I yanked open the door.

She stood outside at the top of the stairs that led up to my place. Her smile was small, a little uncertain. "Can I come in?"

"Sure." I stepped back without thinking and she drifted

past me. Her perfume was musky and floral and familiar. The scent tickled my senses and my dick.

Damn it.

"Cute place." She turned to me as I closed the door.

My gaze dragged down her body. She wore a black, expensive trench coat and spiky black heels. When our eyes locked, Cassie's heated expression put me on alert.

"I hope you don't mind, but Mr. Ironside gave me your address."

"How unprofessional of him," I murmured, my pulse racing.

Her full mouth twitched. "A little." Her fingers toyed nervously with the belt that knotted her coat closed. "Well, I've been thinking all day and ... now I know where I stand, where we stand ... I was ... I was thinking maybe ..." She tugged on the knot and pulled open her coat.

All my blood rushed south.

Cassidy wore a violet satin bra that pushed her already perky breasts up to create very inviting cleavage and matching barely there panties that cut high on her slightly rounded hips. She had definition on her stomach that hadn't been there the last time I'd seen her naked.

For being short, she had long, perfectly formed legs, and right now I wanted those strong, pale thighs wrapped around my hips.

"I was thinking," she continued, shrugging out of the coat, "that sex with you is the best sex I've ever had, and now that I know where we stand, maybe it would be okay if we fucked anytime I visited Ardnoch."

Trying to force rationale past the lust roaring in my head, I replied hoarsely, "Are you sure? I don't want to hurt you."

"I know what this is." She tilted her chin defiantly. "If it gets too much, I'll tell you and we'll stop. Unless ... you don't want to."

My answer was to cross the room and haul her into my arms. Cassie let out a squeal of surprise, but I covered it with my mouth before I carried her into the bedroom. It was clear she'd put some effort into choosing her lingerie for the evening, but I just wanted her naked.

I divested her of the pretty pieces with a speed that had her chuckling in aroused surprise. Then I none too gently threw her on my bed and whipped her heels off, throwing them over my shoulder. My cock strained against my jeans as I gazed down at the beauty sprawled before me. I undressed, devouring her with my eyes. Copper hair billowed around her gorgeous, flushed face, chest rising and falling with arousal, pale pink nipples tight and hard and begging for my mouth. Pretty pussy already wet and ready for me.

Putting a knee to the bed, I climbed over her as I caressed my hand up her smooth leg, trailing my fingertips across her silky inner thigh as she spread to accommodate me. Hovering over her, I reached for her mouth as she reached for mine and kissed her as I slid two fingers inside her wet, tight heat. She was so small, but she'd taken my big cock with eagerness last time.

With her, I didn't feel like she was too fragile, dainty in my arms. Like I could crush her. In fact, I got off on how small she was, how snug she was around my cock, unable to do much but take every inch and enjoy it. I'd always been a dominant bastard in bed, but with Cassie that need was heightened. To claim her. Own her. Make her come so many times she was dripping.

I kissed her deeper, hungrier, and she clung to me with a moan.

I took her pussy in my mouth first. Tonguing and sucking at her clit until her thighs closed around my head and she writhed against me. Deliberately grazing my unshaven cheeks against her skin, I grinned at the cries that accompanied a renewed flush of wet against my tongue. Her musky taste was a fucking addiction.

As Cassie came, I lapped up her climax and tightened my grip on her hips, growling against her pussy as I sucked her swollen clit into my mouth.

She screamed, tugging at my hair, pleading with me as the sensations overwhelmed her. I didn't stop. I didn't stop until she shattered against me again.

Then I moved up and over her, pinning her hands at either side of her head as I nudged my hard, desperate cock between her legs. I held her desire-dazed gaze and pushed inside. So snug, so tight, so swollen. I groaned. "Spread, baby," I commanded gruffly. "Tilt your hips."

Cassie brought her legs around my waist and tilted.

Her inner muscles clutched as I slid all the way in.

"Brock!" Her lips parted on my name and a high gasp, and I felt the sound throb in my cock.

I pulled my hips back, a teasingly slow withdrawal, and then groaned as she squeezed me when I pushed back in.

"Faster," Cassie begged. "Harder."

Balls tightening, I had to force myself not to give in to her pleas.

Instead, I released her hands but only to sit up on my knees, pulling her hips higher, changing the angle of my thrusts. My slow but hard thrusts.

"Oh, Brock." She panted as I dragged out of her painfully, pleasurably, leisurely, until only my tip was inside. Her hands fluttered near her face, eyes sparkling with need, and this overwhelming *feeling* filled my entire chest. I found her swollen clit with my thumb as I moved, and her eyes widened as she tilted her chin back and whimpered.

I circled her clit harder.

"Brock." She gripped the pillow behind her, arching her back. "Harder. Faster."

Desperate for release now, I increased my thrusts, fucking into her, her beautiful tits trembling with my every drive. Her whimpers grew into moans and needy pants, making my balls draw up. I was close. So close.

"Do you like my cock, baby?" I panted as I braced over her, hips snapping as the drive to come overtook everything.

"Yes!" Her nails dug into my back. "I love your cock … ahhhhh!" She threw her head back on a cry of pleasure as I felt her inner muscles throb around me in waves of orgasm.

"Cassie!" I roared as the power of it tore through me, my hips jerking against her as I ground my cock into her, wanting to feel every single lingering, voluptuous tug of her climax.

I fell over Cassie, my lips against her damp skin as I breathed heavily into her neck and shuddered, my cock pulsing and twitching inside her.

Finally, I lifted my head to meet her stunned gaze. "In ten minutes, we're doing that all over again."

Cassidy let out a husky, sexy little laugh. "I think my heart might explode."

Mine too, I thought, covering her mouth with my lips. But not for the reasons she meant.

TEN

CASSIDY

Five months later

Until Brock, I'd never been much of a risk taker. With work, yes. Absolutely. With my heart, no. Never.

So after he told me his story about his ex-wife, about growing up an orphan, I sympathized. I understood why his emotional walls were so high. I didn't have high emotional walls, but there was a security gate with a code, and I was very careful about who I handed that code out to.

That's why going to Brock all those months ago to suggest a casual affair was the riskiest decision I'd ever made. I'd decided life was short and if this was all I could have of him, then I'd take it for as long as my heart would allow it.

Today was my third visit to Ardnoch since we'd started our no-strings-attached affair. I didn't ask him if he was seeing other women when I wasn't around for weeks on end, and he didn't ask if I was seeing other men.

I wasn't.

I didn't want them.

Butterflies started their riotous party in my belly the moment my plane touched down in Inverness. I'd been on a press junket for the past week and looking forward to some R & R in the form of the orgasms only Brock could give me.

I wasn't lying when I told him it was the best sex I'd ever had.

The last time I'd visited, we were so hot that as soon as he opened the door to his apartment, we were all over each other. He'd bent me over his small dining table and tore my underwear. We were both fully dressed when he took me, and I swear all of his neighbors must have heard him bellow as he came. I'd savored the way he'd pushed my hair off my nape and kissed me there before whispering, "Best fucking sex of my life. Always. With you."

And that would have to be enough.

These were my thoughts as Nicole drove the Range Rover we'd borrowed from the estate into Ardnoch.

Watts had gotten out of prison early for good behavior three months ago. There had been nothing. No letters. No emails. No social media comments. Nothing. A huge part of me wanted to hope that he'd learned his lesson, but I was still on high alert. And so was Nicole. She insisted on driving me to Brock's apartment. He'd take me back to the estate. I was pretty sure his colleagues (and the entire village) knew we were fucking, but I didn't care.

Ardnoch villagers protected the privacy of the celebrities who lived on the edges of their lives because our very existence brought in big tourism, which boosted their economy. That meant my dalliance with my ex-bodyguard had not made the tabloids. Though Nicole had become something of a celebrity, the paps having picked up on her constant presence in my life. Young women online loved that I had a female bodyguard, and there were memes about Nicole's badassery. She took it all in stride.

As for me ... well, her training allowed me to add martial artist to my résumé, so we were only in Ardnoch for a few days before I had to fly to Canada to film a thriller action movie where I played a spy.

Nicole waited for me while I ran up the outer staircase to Brock's cute apartment. I knocked and waited with great anticipation for the sounds of his heavy footfall. But nada.

To be fair, I usually texted him to let him know I was coming, but it was kind of last minute and I wanted to surprise him. Knowing I would be in Canada for three months without seeing him seemed impossible. I needed one more fix before we spent the longest time apart we'd spend since starting this thing.

After another knock and nothing, I hurried downstairs and back into the SUV. "Walker said today was Brock's day off, right?"

Nicole nodded. "Definitely."

I glanced over at the small parking lot opposite the converted stables and spotted Brock's blue Ford pickup. "Car's there."

"Which means he walked to wherever he is." Nicole gestured ahead. "I bet he's at the Gloaming." She referred to the local pub and restaurant. "Want to check?"

"Might as well. If I don't find him there, I'll just call him."

A minute later, Nicole slid the Range Rover into the last empty spot outside the pub. "I'll wait."

The pub, restaurant, and hotel was two hundred years old. At least the pub part was. It had been renovated but still had the original low ceiling with dark beams and a huge hearth at one end, as well as booths and cute little tables and a dark wood bar opposite the entrance. It led through to a restaurant I'd eaten in. The food was good.

I felt gazes on me as I stepped into the pub. It sounded vain, but I was used to it. I was one of those celebrities who had a face you couldn't mistake for anyone else's, so I was easily recognized. It was a little frustrating when I wanted to go about my business with no one noticing.

Like, for instance, when I was searching for the man I was sleeping with, only to find him at the bar flirting with another woman.

Those butterflies went wild for a different reason. I felt sick. Brock had smiled more with me than I'd ever seen. Usually, he was so stoic and broody with everyone else.

But he was chuckling at whatever this woman said.

I didn't recognize her. But she was long-legged in her tight dark jeans. Hiking boots on her feet. Cream knit sweater molded to her curvy waist. It had a deep V-neck that showcased spectacular cleavage from huge breasts.

Her dark hair was swept off her face in a long braid that trailed over one shoulder. She was fresh-faced, curvy, and naturally pretty. She was heartbreakingly everything I always thought was more Brock's type than me. The brunette was grinning at him in obvious invitation.

I suddenly felt very odd, small, and unappealing.

Brock tensed, his back straightening, and he turned his head in my direction.

Though he was good at masking his emotions, I knew he was surprised to see me. He muttered something to the brunette and got up.

I was seconds from bursting into extremely embarrassing tears.

There was no way I could do this. I'd just been fooling myself.

Crossing my arms over my chest defensively, I noted the brunette stare longingly after Brock.

"Hey, you're here." Brock was careful not to touch me in public. "Did you text?"

"No." I glanced past him to the woman again. "Who's she?"

"Just a tourist." He gestured to the door. "Let's go."

Back stiff, I strode outside, my gaze flying to Nicole.

She gave me a thumbs-up as if to say "Am I good to go?" and I shook my head. My friend and bodyguard frowned but stayed put.

"Nicole can leave. I'll drive you back after." Brock rested a hand on my lower back to guide me.

"No." I stepped away from him, my gaze darting around to make sure we were alone. There were some folks wandering around farther away. Out of earshot. "I'm going to head back. Sorry."

He scowled. "I was just talking to her."

I glared. "Flirting with her."

At Brock's annoyed silence, I dared to ask, "How many women are you sleeping with when I'm not around?"

The muscle in his jaw twitched as he glowered down at me. "That's not your right to know, because that's not what we are. We agreed."

Unable to hold his gaze because the burning in my chest was so bad, I knew the hurt was written all over me, I held it together long enough to say, "There isn't anyone else for me. No one."

"Cassie ..." He wrapped my name in a pained whisper.

We'd had our heart-to-heart months ago. I knew where Brock stood. There was no changing his mind. But I think when he'd told me that if anyone could make him want to try a relationship again it would be me, I'd held on to hope that over time, he'd see he needed me as much as I needed him.

Yet seeing him with the brunette ... I realized he wasn't falling in love with me.

In all likelihood, he was growing bored with me.

There was no point in bearing more of my heart to him or trying to talk him into loving me. I had more self-respect than that. "This has to be over," I forced out, still unable to look at him. "I'm sorry. Goodbye." I hurried toward the Range Rover, desperately holding myself together. The time to fall apart was when he wasn't there to witness it.

A firm hand wrapped around my biceps, yanking me back around. "Cassie—"

I had no choice but to meet his gaze. "Brock, please!"

At my tortured words, expression, he released me. Like I'd burned him. "Baby, I'm—"

"Don't. Don't call me *baby*. Don't ... if you care even a little about me, you'll just say goodbye."

He looked away, teeth visibly gritted as he scrubbed a hand over his head. Finally, he bit out, "There's been no one but you since we met. And I wasn't planning on sleeping with anyone while we were doing this thing. Just so you know."

But eventually there would be. And the fact that I thought of him as mine all the while he was flirting with other women ... "I still need to end this."

Our eyes held, and I saw so much roiling in his gaze. In the end, he didn't say goodbye. He just nodded.

So I walked away.

And he didn't stop me.

ELEVEN
CASSIDY

One month later

The character I was playing was a damaged but highly intelligent and fearless spy. She'd been traumatized by the murder of her family when she was a teenager. It fueled her.

It wasn't the same, but I poured my heartbreak over Brock into her, and the director was on cloud nine with my performance. I'm glad she was happy, and I was proud of what I was doing. But it didn't make it any easier going about my day like I wasn't the walking fucking wounded.

I was in a particularly bad mood because it was Halloween. Not only was it the one-year anniversary of the first time Brock and I slept together, but people were acting crazy on set. They were pulling pranks, some were dressed up in costume, and there was just a real lack of focus that was driving me kind of crazy.

I was a major party pooper.

When a break hit, I strode off set, and everyone gave me a wide berth.

Nicole fell into stride with me. "Give me a minute." I waved an aggravated hand at her. "I just need some time alone in my trailer."

She nodded, and I sensed her fall away.

"Boo!" Someone wearing a white sheet with eye holes and carrying a clipboard pounced at me as I opened the door to exit the sound studio.

"Jesus!"

She giggled as she slid past me. "Happy Halloween!"

Go fuck yourself, I snarled internally but willed myself not to say it out loud. All I needed was a reputation for being a bitch on set.

I hoofed it to my trailer after that, because I was seconds from biting off someone's head.

Yanking open the door, I hopped up into the trailer and slammed it shut. I bowed my head, letting the silence wash over me.

Thank God.

Pushing off the door, I walked into the bathroom to take care of business. Washing my hands, I stared at my reflection in the small mirror. Makeup did a great job of covering up the dark circles under my eyes. Sleep had not come easily this past month.

My belly grumbled, at least. I had eaten little the first couple of weeks after I ended things with Brock, though my appetite was slowly but surely coming back. Stepping out of the tiny bathroom, intent on grabbing food from catering, I halted my pursuit at the sight of the stranger in my trailer.

"Oh my God!" I cried out, clutching my chest in fright.

The height and build told me it was a guy.

And he wore a freaking Scream mask. You know the one? Disturbing melted white face with black eyeholes and mouth.

Anger overtook my alarm. "Okay, I'm done with this Halloween shit. Who are you and why are you in my trailer?"

At the same time, he raised a fist clenching a large kitchen knife and whipped off the mask.

Genuine terror froze me in place.

Freddy Watts smirked at me as he dropped the mask. "I missed you."

I searched the space for a weapon, finding none that would prove useful. The trailer was really just a place to relax, go over my lines, and nap. There was little space to maneuver. To get away.

How the hell had Watts gotten past studio security?

"All this time I've been waiting for you to miss me too." Watts took a step toward me, and I backed up. His face suddenly flushed with anger. "But you didn't miss me, Cynthia. You've been fucking your ex-bodyguard!"

"My name is not Cynthia."

"Don't lie to me!" He waved the knife. "You can pretend to be someone you're not, but we both know who you really are. And who you really belong to. I need to show you who you really belong to!" He rushed me.

I grappled with him, trying to avoid the blade. We crashed against the kitchen counters, against the opposite wall, and then I tripped over boots I'd left in the narrow corridor. We both went down, and I heard the knife clatter at my side as Watts released it to pin me on the floor.

His grip was a vise around my wrists as he came over me. "I've got you now, Cynthia," he murmured, and I barely heard it over the rushing of blood in my ears. I could feel him hard against me. Nausea roiled in my stomach. No, No, NO!

For months, this man's very existence had terrorized me. Had changed me!

Yes.

Had changed me.

I would not lie down and take this and wait for him to hurt me or for Nicole to rescue me.

I was stronger now.

With a cry of rage, I pushed and struggled against his weight until he slammed my wrists into the floor and bellowed at me to calm down. Pain shot through my arm from where my wrist bones had made impact, and it stunned me for a second.

"Good." Watts groaned and buried his lips against my neck as he ground his erection into me. "I love you, Cynthia."

Hatred and fury burned hotter than ever. "Get off me!" I screamed. "I'm not Cynthia, you sick motherfucker, and I will never be yours!"

It happened so quickly.

He released my right wrist to reach for the knife.

The burning, agonizing pain flared through my abdomen as he stuck it into me twice.

Watts's face was a mask of madness, desire, and bloodlust. "That should shut you up." He dropped the knife beside us again and reached for the zipper of his jeans. "Should keep you quiet while I make love to you."

Wet, hot liquid saturated my T-shirt.

Blood.

Surreal. It felt like I wasn't really in this moment.

But I was in this moment. This awful thing was really happening to me. Dazed, in shock, I had only one thought.

If I was going to die, I was taking the bastard with me.

I screamed like a raging banshee and used every ounce of my strength left to grab the knife and slam it into his gut. I roared my wrath and pulled the knife out, all the while screaming. Then I plunged it again. On that thrust, I left the blade in him.

His face slackened with shock, and his hands fumbled for the knife handle, but all the strength left his body. He slumped, eyelids fluttering shut. Somehow, I pushed him off me despite the weakness filling my own limbs.

Scrambling from under him, I crawled toward the door, leaving blood smears all over the trailer floor and kitchen cupboards. The last thing I remembered was fumbling to get the door open and falling as it swung outward.

TWELVE

BROCK

"You've been a moodier bastard than usual." One of the footmen slapped me on the back as he took a seat at the table behind mine.

The staff room at the estate was fairly quiet as I took a coffee break. I'd been in desperate search for peace for a month.

It wasn't happening.

And not just because the castle was abuzz with plans for their Halloween party, but because I missed Cassidy Ward with every inch of my fucking being. It was worse this time around than last.

Walker had told me she canceled her membership.

She wasn't coming back.

Now there was no reason for me to stay.

I was already looking at other job opportunities. Maybe one that would take me to LA. Or New York.

Masochistic bastard that I was, I was greedy for just one more moment with Cassie.

When she walked away, I hadn't realized what that truly meant. Until I discovered she'd canceled her membership.

So, aye, I suppose I was more of a brooding bastard than usual.

I didn't reply, just sipped at my coffee and stared balefully at the TV screen. The news was playing on low.

When the chyron on the screen displayed Cassidy's name, as if plucking her from my thoughts, I lunged for the remote and bumped up the volume.

The female news presenter announced, "And in other news, actor Cassidy Ward, famous for playing genius mathematician Cynthia Riley on the hit show *The Female Quotient*, is in critical condition in a Vancouver hospital. The actor was filming in British Columbia when she was attacked in her trailer. Her assailant, thirty-five-year-old Freddy Watts, has also been admitted to hospital. Reports suggest he and Ward suffered multiple stab wounds in the altercation. Ward's battle with stalker Freddy Watts hit the news last summer ..."

Ice-cold terror washed over me.

"Brock?"

I dropped the remote and ran from the room, following the corridor to Walker's office. Barging in without knocking, I demanded of my boss, "I need to get to Vancouver. Now."

Ironside stared stonily back at me. "Why? What's going on?"

With more calm than I felt, I relayed what had happened to Cassidy. I'd barely finished and Walker was on his phone, making a call for me.

It took everything within me to stand still and wait. And to not throw up. I'd been in war zones. I'd been shot at, stabbed, fucking faced the worst monsters this world had to offer.

But the fear of losing Cassidy and knowing I'd lost her because not only was I a coward but because I wasn't there to protect her ... well, fuck ... that was the worst monster I knew I'd ever face.

Thirteen

Cassidy

The first person I saw when I woke up, disoriented, in what was obviously a hospital room, was Brock.

The beeping from the machines hooked up to me was grating, the light was too bright, and there was a dull pain in my abdomen.

But Brock was here.

Why?

I gazed blearily at his face, still frowning in sleep as he sat sprawled awkwardly in a hospital chair by the bed. Longing gave way to memories, and flashes of my battle with Watts flooded in.

Whimpering, I heard the beeping grow faster.

Brock's eyes flew open and there was no sign of his weariness as relief etched into his features. "Baby ..." His voice was hoarse with emotion as he leaned over, grabbing my hand to press a kiss to the back of it. "You're awake."

"Y-you're here." Why was he here?

Tears suddenly brightened his eyes, and I think I was more shocked by that than waking up in a hospital bed. "I thought I'd lost you for good."

What did that mean?

"Watts?" I croaked out.

"Dead." Brock growled, and I saw the savage satisfaction he took in those words.

I did not take savage satisfaction in the fact that I'd killed my attacker. But I also refused to feel guilt after everything that evil man had put me through. I was too tired for guilt.

"I'll get the doctor." Brock stood before I could ask any more questions.

A while later, after a chat with the doc about how I was a miracle and how Watts hadn't punctured any vital organs but I'd lost a lot of blood, that my recovery looked good ... Nicole came in before Brock and I could talk again. She looked ravaged with guilt, and I spent some time reassuring her she was the reason I was alive. She'd taught me to fight back and she'd made me strong, both physically and mentally.

Mom's flight had been delayed, so I talked to her on the phone. She was frantic, but I assured her I was okay.

There were others. My agent. Cast and crew from the movie. But Brock could see how weary I was, as could the nursing staff. They insisted everyone go home.

Brock stayed.

When I woke up a few hours later, he was still there.

His eyes were on me as I blinked open to wakefulness.

"I should have been there to protect you. I am so sorry, baby." His voice shook. "You'll never know how much."

I didn't want him to be in pain with regret. Reaching out a hand to him, he took it, pressing kisses against the back of it. "Brock ... I don't blame you. And honestly, I'm proud of myself. I think I needed to be the one who faced him. I needed to know I could do it. That I'll never need anyone else to make me feel safe."

Brock leaned forward, eyes searing with emotion. "I still want to be the man who makes you feel safe."

My breath caught. "What does that mean?"

"I'm done being a coward. I want to be brave so I'm worthy of you. I ... I love you so much, Cassidy Ward. Every day without you has been agony. I thought ... When I heard the news, I thought my punishment for being a coward was to lose you before I could tell you how I feel."

Tears spilled freely down my cheeks. "Really?"

"Aye, really." He swept them away with his thumb. "Do you forgive me?"

I nodded, sobbing.

"Do you think you might love me back?"

I laughed at the ridiculous question, and it hurt. "Ow."

"Shit. Please be careful." He brushed his lips over mine.

"I love you, Brock. I've never stopped loving you."

Brock squeezed his eyes closed in relief and then couldn't resist kissing me a little longer, a little harder. My fingers slid into his hair to hold him close. Finally, he broke the kiss to whisper a vow in my ear, "I won't ever leave you again."

EPILOGUE

The news presenter finished relaying the latest from the Scottish government, her serious face giving way to a small smile. "And in other news, the village of Ardnoch is buzzing with activity this weekend as tourists and media descend to celebrate the wedding of Emmy Award-winning actor Cassidy Ward. The actor and her husband-to-be, Brock McIntosh, became internet favorites when their romance went public two years ago after Ward recovered from a brutal attack by stalker Freddy Watts. Ward famously fell in love with her Scottish bodyguard, and it's fair to say the public has fallen in love with their romance.

"The pair are holding their wedding reception at the famous Ardnoch Estate. It's not the first celebrity wedding the estate has hosted, but it's unusual for them to decide to marry at the village church. Tourists are excited to see the loved-up couple make their way into the church, and it seems like the villagers are getting into the spirit of the event. Our entertainment correspondent, Maggie Ivers, is in Ardnoch this afternoon. Maggie, what is the atmosphere like right now up there in Ardnoch?"

"Well, Hannah, no one likes a wedding better than the Scots, but I get the sense from talking with locals and tourists that this one is extra special. Not just because one of our own is getting married, but because we love a good happily ever after. And there's a genuine feeling here that Cassidy Ward deserves all the happiness in the world. She inspires a lot of respect and goodwill. Two years on and fans are still reeling from her attack, proud of her for the work she's doing campaigning for better laws against stalking, and if I might say, pleased as punch she's come out stronger than ever after her ordeal. There's a lot of joy here for the happy couple, Hannah. Not to sound like a cheesy song, but you can really feel the love in the air."

"It sounds wonderful. I wish I were there."

"We wish you were here too. I'll be back tomorrow with live updates from the wedding."

"We're all looking forward to it, Maggie."

"Bye for now from Ardnoch."

The Highlands Series Bonus Scenes

WALKER

Ardnoch, Scottish Highlands
October

Impatience rode my shoulders.

Now that we'd decided we were doing this, I wanted it done.

I wanted Sloane to be my wife.

Hard to believe that the very thought would have sent me running this time last year. Now I couldn't be without her.

"You look angry."

I turned my head ever so slightly toward my best man. Brodan's lips pressed tightly together to suppress a smile. The grin broke free at whatever he saw in my expression.

"You are a very angry-looking man right now." He waved a finger at my face. "You might want to do something about that before the bride makes an appearance."

"I'm not angry. I'm ecstatic," I replied tonelessly.

"Aye, you're definitely not reading ecstatic." He reached up and pushed a finger against the corners of my mouth. "Try something like that."

"Fuck off," I muttered under my breath, swatting his hands away. "Sloane knows the difference between my angry face and happy face."

"If you say so."

"Are all best men as annoying as you?" I asked, my gaze roaming the small group of guests seated in front of us.

"They're certainly less expensive. You know, people would pay to have me be their best man at their wedding." Brodan winked at his wife, Monroe. She sat in the front row with their baby boy, Lennox, sleeping against her chest. Brodan winked at her, and she rolled her eyes.

"I feel like I'm paying," I retorted. "And that I've been shortchanged."

Brodan chuckled, clapping me on the back. "You know, you've gotten funny since you met Sloane."

I grunted and my friend laughed harder.

My mum and dad sat in the front row, along with Monroe and baby Nox. On the bride's side sat Aria Howard, Sloane's ex-boss and newly found friend. Brodan's family had sat on either side, since neither Sloane—nor I — had much in the way of family and friends. We were building that together, here in Ardnoch.

We could have invited more of the village, considering Sloane's new bakery business had taken off and people here knew her well. But a month ago, after weeks of wedding planning with her friends, Sloane had confessed to me she just wanted a small, private ceremony and reception. That what mattered more to her was just being married to me.

Considering I would run away with her to get married at the registry office in a heartbeat, I'd agreed with the change of plans. Brodan's brothers Lachlan and Arran owned the local pub and hotel, the Gloaming. They'd agreed to close the reception rooms for the day so we could get married there.

We'd hired a humanist since neither of us were particularly

religious and Sloane had slimmed her bridal party down to two.

It would just be her and her daughter, Callie. An eleven-year-old sweetheart of a kid, who I vowed to love as my own.

I was impressed by what Sloane pulled off in just four weeks with the decorating and organizing. The Gloaming was decked out for the wedding, her touch everywhere. Wee lanterns and fairy lights, white silk cotton, twigs sprayed in glitter for some reason. Autumn colored flowers. Nothing overtly showy. It worked.

A sudden song transition on the PA system made me straighten, my pulse picking up speed. It wasn't my kind of music, but Sloane had played the tune to me a few weeks ago. It was called Carry You by people I'd never heard of. Ruelle and Flurry or Fleurie or some such thing.

I wasn't one to get emotional about much, let alone a song, but when we sat together in our home listening to lyrics, I got a wee bit choked up.

If a song could be perfect for us, I suppose that was it.

But even if I'd hated the track, I'd have gone along with it.

I just wanted Sloane happy. I didn't care about weddings and decoration and menus. All I cared about was becoming her husband.

The haunting voices sang words that meant something to us and suddenly Callie appeared in the doorway between the dining room/converted ceremony room and the pub beyond it. She looked like the wee angel that she was in a pale pink flower girl dress. Her eyes met mine and she beamed, throwing white rose petals from the basket she carried in her hand as she strolled down the aisle. Catching sight of her best friend, Lewis Adair, she gave him a quick, excited wave and he gave her a cool kid nod back.

Then her gaze returned to meet mine and she grinned at me. Emotion suddenly gleamed in her eyes and she hurried the last few steps to throw her arms around me, the now empty basket banging against my back.

I bent over slightly, hugging her tightly to me, feeling an overwhelming wave of love and protectiveness come over me. Stroking a hand down her carefully arranged hair, I whispered, "We all good, wee yin?"

Callie pulled away slightly, craning her neck back. She blinked rapidly, as if embarrassed by her tears.

Stroking a thumb over her cheek, I said, "Big day, eh? You look beautiful, wee yin."

She smiled, lips trembling. "Wait until you see mom."

I took her hand and pulled her into my side, instead of letting her go to stand on the bride's side. Callie hugged into me as my gaze met *my* mum's.

Tears spilled down her cheeks and she patted at them hurriedly, as if she, too, was embarrassed by the emotion. Dad gripped her free hand tight in his.

My reconciliation with my parents was a slow and ongoing process.

But I was glad they were here.

Callie's hand tightened around mine, drawing my gaze up toward the door.

Sloane stood at the top of the aisle and my breath caught at the sight of her.

My pulse throbbed in my throat as she made her way toward me.

I wasn't the best with words. All I knew was that the woman walking toward me, who I loved more than I'd loved anyone, was the classiest and yet sexiest bride I'd ever seen in my life.

The dress had a lace overlay thing and lace slaves that fell down her arms. They made me think of undressing her. Her perfect collarbone and shoulders were bare, and the neckline hugged the curves of her breasts in a heart shape. The bodice was tight-fitting, and the rest flowed into a skirt and train that made her look like a real-life princess.

She'd pulled her hair back in a simple ponytail and she wore the pearl and diamond earrings I'd given her as a wedding gift.

Stunning.

Inside and out.

And she wanted to marry me.

"She looks like a princess." Callie grinned up at me.

"Aye, she does that." I looked back at Sloane, whose gaze was on mine and Callie's joined hands. A sheen of tears covered her eyes as ours met.

When she reached us, the music stopped, and she shifted her bouquet to one hand and held out the other to Callie. "We should do this together."

I nodded and fell into place beside my bride, with our daughter between us. "You look incredible," I told Sloane.

She grinned. "You look so handsome." Her eyes dropped to Callie, who looked between us like Christmas had arrived early this year. "And you look adorable."

"Let's do this," Callie announced, facing the humanist.

Sloane's soft laughter made me feel like I was floating outside of myself.

It might never feel comfortable to experience the happiness I'd long thought I didn't deserve.

Maybe I never would.

But discomfort in happiness was a small price to pay to have Sloane and Callie in my life forever.

"Honored guests," the humanist, an older woman named Marie who'd traveled from Inverness, greeted the room. "We gather here today to witness the marriage between this man and this woman. Fate brought Sloane Harrow and Walker Ironside beyond an ocean to meet. Fate was not always kind and those of you who join us today, being closest to the happy couple, know better than most that Sloane and Walker had to fight significant obstacles to be here today. But here they stand. Together. Celebrating their loving union.

"In getting to know Sloane and Walker, I learned Walker is a man of few words. A man of action."

I heard Brodan grunt with amusement and shot him a look that only made him grin harder.

"So it will come as no surprise that Walker and Sloane will make their vows later in private and wish for a brief ceremony. Probably the shortest ceremony of my career," Marie joked.

I shrugged as Callie giggled.

Sloane knew I loved her. I didn't need to say so in front of all these people. She knew me so well. She was the one who suggested we give our vows in private.

"Without further ado: Do you, Walker Ironside, take this woman, Sloane Harrow, to be your wife?"

"I do."

Callie squeezed my hand hard.

"And do you, Sloane Harrow, take this man, Walker Ironside, to be your husband?"

"I do."

Marie gestured with open arms. "I now pronounce you husband and wife. You may kiss the bride."

"That's my cue to leave!" Callie cried cutely as she released our hands and skittered back, grinning mischievously.

Everyone laughed and though it trembled on my lips, I wanted to savor the good part. I pulled Sloane into my arms, feeling her familiar softness against me as I cupped her nape in my palm to crush her mouth to mine.

Then I bent her with a flourish that made the room erupt into cheers and I felt Sloane's laughter against my lips as she clung to me.

I broke the kiss, grinning down at her. "To make up for the vows."

She bent her hand back in laughter as I pulled her back upward, off her feet, to kiss her again. Sloane peppered me in hard, quick, happy kisses until I gently lowered her to her feet.

Brodan clapped me on the back, but for now I ignored him, eyes only for my wife.

My wife.

I cupped her beautiful face in my hands. "Sloane Ironside."

Her eyebrows rose in question.

"I just wanted to hear how it sounds."

She beamed. "It sounds damn good."

"It sounds right." Our gazes held and I murmured, "I love you, Sloane Ironside."

"I love you too, husband."

SLOANE

WHILE I WAS A LITTLE TIPSY AND TEARFUL TO SAY goodbye to Callie, she seemed more than happy to leave with the Adairs for her sleepover at Lewis's.

Walker and I were not far behind her, however, leaving the Gloaming with the last of our small group of guests to walk home. Our house was only a few minutes' drive from the center of the village, but we'd both been drinking, so we decided to walk the ten minutes home.

I'd changed out of my wedding dress into a sixties style off-white mini with a lace overlay that mimicked my wedding gown. Walker appeared ready to eat me alive, his gaze constantly dipping to my bare legs.

My skin was flushed with champagne, and I was a little

loopy with it, but still completely cognizant. I wanted to remember my wedding. It might have been small, but it was full of so much joy and contentment.

I curled my arm around Walker's, burying into his side as we walked home through the quiet streets. My heeled boots echoed off the cobbled roads as I took in the faint glow of the Victorian street lights against the sandstone buildings. The old part of the village was so beautiful. Even on a slightly dreary October evening.

"Cold?" he asked.

I shook my head before resting it on his shoulder.

"Happy?"

"So happy. I might die from it."

He gave a huff of amusement. "I know what you mean."

With the silence of the beautiful village surrounding us, I decided now was as good a time as any to deliver my vows. "Walker Ironside, I vow to love you through sickness and health, through kidnappings and car crashes—"

He shook with laughter, and I smacked his thick biceps playfully.

"Through gunshot wounds—though no more of those, please—through inheritance schemes, and the pre-teen/teen years we're about to experience with Callie. I vow to love you through whatever life throws at us because I know together we can handle anything. You're my protector, but I'm yours, too. And I vow to protect your heart and soul and body for the rest of my life."

Walker stopped abruptly and kissed me, desperately, almost painfully. Our breathing was quick and shallow as he pulled back, my face clasped in his palms. "I'm not as good with words as you are, Sloane. Though I hope by now you know how much I love you."

I nodded, smiling. I knew. It was in everything he did for me and for Callie. The man had taken a literal bullet for me.

"I vow to love you forever. And I vow to love Callie forever."

Tears filled my eyes.

"I vow to be the father that wee girl deserves. I vow that with every fiber of my very being."

A tear slipped free, and Walker caught it on his thumb.

"I want to adopt her, Sloane. I want her to be mine. Officially."

The sob burst forth before I could stop it and I buried my face in his chest, probably covering his tux in makeup, but I couldn't care. "I—I d-didn't think it was possible to get any happier!" I said the last word on a whiny sob that made Walker shake with more laughter.

"Is this happiness? You promise?"

Laughing through my tears, I pulled away to nod. "So happy. Callie is going to feel so loved. She loves you so much already as the dad she's never had."

"I want to start the process now. It can take a while. But with Nathan in prison partly because he kidnapped and terrorized his own daughter, I don't see how the court will have a problem with granting me the adoption. Still, I thought we'd wait to tell Callie until it's official."

"That makes sense." I shook my head as I pushed him away, teasing. "The guy doesn't have words, but he still manages to one up me on the vows."

Walker flashed me that rare smile.

I sighed in pretend weariness. "I guess being the loser means being the one who gets tied up tonight." When was I not the one who got tied up? Still, Walker's eyes flashed with heat. "Maybe I'll even let you put me across your knee."

The words were barely out of my mouth before I found myself swooped up and thrown over Walker's shoulder. I cried out in hysterical laughter, clinging onto his broad shoulders for dear life as he started running through the streets of Ardnoch.

"Men!" I cackled.

"Shh, you'll wake everyone up." He smacked my ass and I let out a huff of excitement.

"Yeah, run faster."

We didn't make it to the bedroom when we stumbled into our house. Walker lowered me to my feet and fucked me against the front door.

The tying up and ass smacking came later that night, and I came too many times to count.

Later, in the wee hours of the morning, deliciously aching between my thighs from being well-used by my husband, I curled up in his arms and whispered, "That's the first time I've ever had sex as someone's wife." My rings glittered on my hand where it laid on his powerful chest. "Was it just me or was the sex impossibly better?"

Walker trailed a lazy hand down my spine. "It was definitely better."

"It was nice we could be so loud... but the house feels empty without Callie."

"Agreed." He pressed a kiss to my forehead. "We'll sleep for a bit and then go pick her up for some breakfast. As for being loud... we'll find our times. We've got our honeymoon to look forward to."

I nodded, snuggling deeper into him. "Good night, Husband."

Walker's voice was gruff as he replied, "Sweet dreams. Wife."

Aria

Ardnoch Estate, Scottish Highlands

"Do you know how it looks if you do not have an engagement party? It says you do not believe this is a relationship that is going to last, *tesoro*. You are saying that you are ashamed of North which makes no sense."

I rolled my eyes because my mother couldn't see me doing it. Then I gestured to Maya, the interior design professional we'd hired to come up from Edinburgh to decorate the castle for Christmas. "Mamma," I said in a placating voice as I wrinkled my nose at the extra garland Maya was directing her staff to put on the fireplace mantel in the great hall.

Too much? She mouthed.

I nodded.

"Tesoro?"

"Mamma, I'm kind of in the middle of work right now but all I can say is that not having an engagement party doesn't say any of those things. All it says is that North and I are feeling very private right now. After what we've been through this year, I think people will find it entirely understandable."

"Sometimes it is like you were not even raised in my world," my mother huffed dramatically down the line. "We need to host an engagement party. It has been two months since the engagement!"

"Yeah exactly. It'll be the wedding soon enough so why bother wasting money on a party that North nor I want?" I gasped, seeing the lights for the huge tree in the great hall come on. "Oh it's beautiful." I smiled appreciatively at Maya.

"You are being rude, Aria," my mom cried in her musical Italian accent.

"I'm at work. We'll talk about this later. Bye, Mamma." I hung up on her spluttering protests.

Maya glanced at me giving me a sympathetic smile. "Mothers."

"Oh you have no idea." My phone buzzed in my hand and I saw it was a call from one of the bands we were auditioning for the Christmas party. "Are you good here?"

"We're good. We can make any adjustments you're not sure of later." She shooed me away. "Go work."

Ten minutes later, I'd talked to the band, and then gotten another call from a club member's PA regarding the room they *demanded* during their stay at Christmas. I'd just gotten off that call when my phone rang again and it was my little sister, Allegra.

I answered but put her on speaker so I could deal with the emails piling up in my inbox. "How goes it, Ally?"

"I'm coming directly to Scotland for Christmas and I just told Mamma and she's pissed so expect a call. I'm really sorry. I told her not to bother you with it."

Groaning inwardly, I tried to concentrate on my emails and handle this conversation but I couldn't. "Why can't you go home at Christmas break and just fly over here with Mamma and Dad on Christmas Eve?"

That was the original plan. They'd spend the holidays with me and North but stay at their beach house on the estate. North and I had bought the beach house two doors down from them so it wasn't like they wouldn't see us all the time. I'd moved out of my parents' vacation home on the estate and into ours just two weeks ago. Sadly, North hadn't spent a night in the house with me yet. He was in Glasgow working on a TV show. I'd been trying to fly down and visit him every weekend but it hadn't been possible these past few. We hadn't seen each other since I moved into the house and I missed him so badly it was almost alarming. The place didn't feel like ours yet because he wasn't there to enjoy it with me.

Allegra groaned. "Because I don't want to spend any time in LA and Mamma doesn't seem to understand that. I have two weeks off from school and I want to spend them in Scotland. Don't you want me there? Oh God, like, am I intruding on you and North?"

It wasn't that I didn't want my little sister here with me for the holidays but it would cause drama with our mother and Christmas was going to be the first real time North and I had together in two months.

"Of course not. You know you're welcome to stay with us."

"No, I'll stay at our house so I'm not in your way. I'm just sorry it's causing drama. But I'm sure Gail told you what she told me: I can't adjust my actions to placate Mamma."

After I'd been kidnapped by my old friend, Caitlyn Branch, Allegra had insisted I started video sessions with her therapist Gail. She had in fact said something similar to me about Mamma. "I know you're right. I just... she's on my back about a stupid engagement party, I'm—" a knock sounded at my office door cutting me off. "Come in!"

The head butler, Wakefield, stepped into the room. "I'm sorry to interrupt, Ms. Howard, but the electrician and the interior designer are uh..." he cleared his throat, expression carefully blank, "In *discussions* regarding how many lights can be strung in the dining room. Some members are complaining about the volume of the discussion."

I gave him a tight smile, feeling my blood pressure rise. "I'll be right there." I stood up as he departed. "Allegra, I need to call you back."

"Don't forget to! I want to talk to you about possibly transferring to school in Scotland."

I froze on the spot. "What?"

But she'd already hung up.

Twenty minutes later, I'd barely returned to my office after playing referee between the electrician and Maya. Of course I had to side with my electrician for the safety of our guests, leaving Maya nonplussed that her 'design would just have to change then'. I politely suggested she have a late lunch and take time to think about it while I escaped.

I had not eaten lunch and I was getting hangry.

My phone had buzzed constantly in the last twenty minutes and a glance at it told me it was missed calls from my mother, text messages from her and companies I was coordinating efforts with for the Christmas Party, and another apology text from Allegra along with the reminder to call her back.

I'd barely opened up my emails when another knock sounded on my office door. Gritting my teeth, I called come in and Jock, my head of security, strolled in. "Ms. Howard."

It was not Jock's fault that my family were driving me crazy, that my job was raising my blood pressure, or that none of it seemed as manageable as it used to be because I missed not having North around to vent to on the daily. "What can I do for you, Jock?"

He gave me a half grimace half smile. "Unfortunately, despite our previous conversations on appropriate placement, some of the decorations that have gone up today are interfering with the feeds on our security cameras."

Maya had ignored Jock's instructions, it seemed. I hung my head with a groan at the thought of asking Maya to move them.

"Sorry."

Waving my hand at him, I reluctantly stood. "Not your fault. It's just my interior designer is a little temperamental today. Can you show me where the issues are?"

Thirty minutes later, I slumped back into my seat and had only answered one email when my computer started ringing.

Seeing it was North calling to video chat, I answered even though I had a gazillion things to do.

North's handsome face appeared on my computer screen. He gave me a sexy, tender smile. "Hi, Gorgeous."

"Hey," the word came out half-croak, half-whine.

North instantly frowned. "What's going on? You look frazzled."

"Babe, that is an understatement."

"Talk to me."

So I did. I vented until I was flushed and agitated all over again. North instructed me to send for something to eat from the kitchen while he distracted me with tales of his day on set. I wished for the millionth time he was here in person. Dealing with my family and with my job just seemed so much less overwhelming when I knew he was there to go home to at the end of the day.

AT LUNCH TIME THE NEXT DAY, WAKEFIELD knocked on my door. There was an amused gleam in his eyes as he cleared his throat. "Ms. Howard, your presence is requested in the Bruce Suite."

I frowned. "Why?"

"An issue, I'm told. I'm not sure of the details."

Nonplussed I nodded absently as I turned back to my screen. "Let me just finish this email."

"It is rather urgent, I'm told."

Suspicious, I sent the email and narrowed my eyes on the butler. "And yet you don't know why I'm needed in the suite?"

He returned my skeptical gaze with a bland one. "No, Ms. Howard."

I knew something fishy was up but still I let Wakefield lead me out of my office and through the castle toward the staff elevator. The sight of the decorations and lights cheered me somewhat. Ardnoch was magical at this time of year.

When Wakefield got on the elevator with me, I raised a brow. "You're coming with me then?"

"As head butler I should be aware of any possible issues with the guests too, no." Was his only answer.

Hmm.

My eyes remained narrowed on his back as he led me off the lift and down the corridor toward one of the castle's bigger suites. Wakefield opened the bedroom door with a flourish and gestured me inside. At the small smile twitching his lips, I knew something was definitely up.

Striding inside, I came to a stop at the sight of a laptop open on the bed. North's face filled the screen. Beside the bed was a Butler's cart with covered dishes and a bottle of champagne in an ice bucket.

"What on earth..."

"Hi, gorgeous," North grinned on the screen. "Wakefield helped me set up this wee surprise. I thought you deserved something a bit special this week and just because I can't be there physically, doesn't mean I can't enjoy a romantic lunch with my fiancée."

Love and tenderness filled me as I beamed back at North. Wakefield appeared at the butler's cart and lifted the largest cloche. "Two house cheeseburgers and truffle fries."

I laughed at North's choice because he knew me so well.

Wakefield returned the cloche and lifted the smaller one. "Two slices of salted caramel chocolate torte."

"How on earth am I going to eat all of this?" I snorted. "Did you really need to serve two of everything?"

"Aye." North spoke instead. "It's got to be like I'm actually there."

"It's a terrible waste."

My fiancé narrowed his eyes. "You're ruining the pretense."

Giggling, I attempted to look apologetic and failed. "I'm very sorry."

North looked at the butler. "That will be all, Wakefield. Thank you for your help."

"You're most welcome, Mr. Hunter." He bowed his head and then nodded to me with that amusement still glittering in his eyes before he departed the room.

As soon as the door closed behind him, I sat on the bed, pulling the laptop near. "I can't believe you did all this."

"You sounded stressed yesterday." The screen bobbed as if North was moving and I realized he was using green screen for his background. It looked like he was walking through a jungle.

"Why the green screen?" I chortled.

"Because I'm walking through my rental and it's a shithole and I don't want you to know how much of a slob I am when you're not here."

I narrowed my eyes. "That doesn't sound like you."

North cocked his head. "Did you hear that?"

I glanced away from the screen. "Hear what?"

A knock sounded on the bedroom door a second before it opened.

And standing on the threshold was my fiancé.

I flew off the bed with a cry of delight and threw myself into North's arms. He stumbled back on impact, laughing as he embraced me.

"Well, that is a nice, bloody welcome," he murmured gruffly in my ear.

Even as I inhaled his familiar scent and drank in his warmth, I pulled back just enough to ask, "How … when… what?"

North chuckled, his hands resting just above my ass. "The director wants to do some rewrites. I didn't think I was needed there but I got the feeling I was needed here so I've come up for a long weekend."

Pleasure filled me. "You're here for three nights?"

"I'm here for three nights. Already dropped my bags off at the house."

"I can't believe you did this." I gestured around us.

His expression sobered. "No matter where I am, or what I'm doing, if you need me I will always drop everything to be there. Don't you know that by now?"

Emotion thickened my throat. "As much as I appreciate the gesture, you don't need to come running every time I'm a little stressed out."

A cocky glint entered his eyes. "Well considering I am your destressing tool, I humbly disagree."

Heat flashed through me. "Oh yeah? What kind of destressing did you have in mind?"

"I thought I might fuck you til' you see stars," he murmured against my mouth.

Pulse racing, I nodded, pulling him toward the bed. "Lunch can wait."

His grin was smug and sexy and made thighs clench together as he laid me down on the bed and braced over me. "Naughty Ms. Howard, playing hooky with her members."

I huffed. "One member." I slid my hand down his stomach to grasp him through his jeans. He was already hard. Not that it was a surprise. "This one."

North half-groaned, half-chuckled at my innuendo. "Two weeks without you is too long, gorgeous."

"For me too." I yanked him down to my mouth, my words a little breathless. "Now make it up to me, Mr. Hunter. And I'd quite like it if you called me Mrs. Hunter while you do it."

Heat and possessiveness darkened his expression seconds before he crushed his mouth to mine. North's kiss always had the ability to plunge me into somewhere else. Somewhere better. Safe. Hot. Sexy. Needful.

As I wrapped my arms around him, kissing him back with all my worth, I knew deep in my bones that I had something so few people ever got to experience. And if a few weeks apart every now and then reminded me of how special our bond was... I could live with that.

Sarah

There was only a slight chill in the air, the sun shining brightly above our heads as we drove up the winding road toward Through the Glen Cottage. Even so, the mountains in the distance wore beautiful snowy hats, reminding us that winter was coming.

"I know it's stunning up here this time of year," Theo said as we pulled into our driveway. "But I was thinking it might make more sense for us to spend the summer and autumn here and head back to London for winter, since it's a smidgeon warmer there."

The suggestion made sense and I truly didn't mind what time of year we spent here, as long as I got to spend half my time in the Highlands. "I'm happy to do that."

We'd just spent two weeks with Jared, catching up with Aria and Allegra and all our friends, before jumping in the car to spend the next few months in Gairloch.

We'd spent the past two years bouncing between London, Dundee, Ardnoch and Gairloch. The Juno McLeod series was filmed partly in Dundee and had finished its first season and was an international success and critical acclaim. My book sales had skyrocketed and fans had even recognized me out and about. Olivia Jones, who played Juno, was very much expected to be nominated in next January's award season, as were Theo and the rest of the cast and writers. Since I was a co-writer on the show, that included me.

The thought of adding an Emmy or Golden Globe nomination to the list of surreal things that had happened to me in the last few years was just a wee bit too much for me to wrap my head around. In fact, I was very much looking forward to not thinking about any of it for another few days. Theo and I had agreed to just enjoy each other before we launched back into work. I needed to start the next book in the series, and would also be involved in our video calls with a small team of writers we'd brought on board for the show going forward.

For now, we'd enjoy a few days of nothing but peace, the beach, good food and each other's company.

Theo grabbed my luggage and his while I ran ahead to let us into the cottage. My first stop was switching on the heating and the gas fire in the living room. As soon as the flames flickered to life, I turned to stare out of the large window that framed the most stunning view of the loch. I released a breath I didn't even know I'd been holding.

"Glad to be home?" Theo asked as he wandered in, dumping the bags so he could shut the door.

I smiled over at him. "Very."

He crossed the rooms to pull me into his arms, his chin resting on the top of my head as he gazed out the window. "It's rather a difficult view to beat, isn't it?"

"There's nothing quite like it." I snuggled against him, truly content in a way I didn't even know was possible.

We spent the rest of the afternoon unpacking and then did a quick run to the grocery store to get some supplies. Everything had been comfortable and lovely between us all day, but I noted a tension rise in Theo as he cooked dinner. He'd grown quiet in a brooding way I could sense, even though he wasn't saying much. We just knew each other so well now that I detected even the slightest change in his demeanor.

We sat across from each other at the dining table, the gas fire still blazing to ward off the chill and casting a warm glow across the dimly lit room. Theo ate slowly, staring at his plate, having said barely a word since we sat down.

Confused, I attempted to recall our conversations today and whether anything was said that could have upset him.

Nothing came to mind.

"Do you think you might tell me what's wrong?" I asked after swallowing a bite of the steak he'd cooked.

Theo finally glanced up from his plate, his expression bored. "Nothing's wrong."

True concern lit through me because we were well past him withholding his feelings from me. "Then you're doing an awfully good job of pretending there's a problem."

He sighed. Heavily. "I just... Do you want children?"

I think my eyebrows probably hit my hairline at the abrupt question. "Sorry, what?"

Sitting back, his plate abandoned, Theo considered me. "You realize in the two years we've been dating, neither of us has brought up the subject of children. And I don't want to sound indelicate, but surely at our age it's something we should discuss."

Heart racing a wee bit faster than before, I nodded. I took a moment to consider my words. Because of course I'd thought about children and whether Theo wanted them. About whether *I* wanted them. The problem was, I was terrified to discover we weren't on the same page about it, so I'd never brought it up.

"I'll do whatever you want," Theo suddenly said, his voice tight with emotion. "I'm not sure what kind of father I'd make, but if you want children, we'll have children. If you don't want children, we won't have children. All I want is you, Sarah."

Emotion thickened in my throat, coming over me so quickly at his gruff words; the love and devotion I heard in them, and saw in his eyes. Tears blurred my vision and when I blinked to clear them, a few escaped. I quickly wiped them away, my heart aching at the worried look on Theo's face.

Putting him out of his misery, I told him, "When I was younger, I always thought I'd be a mum. Like it's built into society so much that girls grow up to be mums, that I never thought that I *wouldn't* be a mum. But I also never really thought about whether I *wanted* to be a mother."

Theo waited.

Guilt flickered through me as it always did when I thought about what I really wanted. Guilt I knew I shouldn't feel, but was there because of the aforementioned societal and genetic pressure to procreate. "I think...I love my life with you as it is. I love we can take off when we want to wherever we want. That we can sleep in when we want. Make love in any room of the house when we want."

Theo's lips quirked up, his eyes glowing as he watched me.

"I would be so happy to spend the rest of my life... just us. I can be a fun aunt to our friend's children, and possibly Jared's if he ever settles down." I grinned at the thought.

"And you're absolutely positive that's what you want?" He leaned forward, searching my face for the truth.

"It's what I want. But I want to make sure that you want that too?"

"I want that too," he promised. "Just you and me."

Relief trickled through me but I pressed, "You said you'd have kids if that's what I wanted…"

He nodded. "Because I'd do anything to keep you. And if a child came into the picture, I'd do my damndest to be a better father than my own. Which wouldn't be hard, I suppose."

"But it wouldn't be your first choice?"

"What can I say?" he shrugged. "I'm a selfish bastard who wants you all to myself. But you knew that already…So we're on the same page?"

"We're on the same page, Mr. Cavendish."

"Good." He stood up abruptly and asked as he marched toward me, "Are you done with that?" Not waiting for my response, he lifted me out of my chair like I weighed nothing.

I squealed in surprise, our laughter mingling as Theo swung me into his arms like I was a bride and strode toward our bedroom.

"Let's fuck just to fuck and not to make a baby," he teased.

"Yes, please!" I cried, charmed by his playfulness, as always.

Theo threw me on the bed, and I had to swat my hair out of my face. My giggles cascaded across us as he climbed over me with an exaggerated growl of want. The teasing nuzzling at my neck quickly ignited into a desire that had not abated in the two years we'd been together.

Maybe it would dampen in time, but the thought didn't fill me with sadness. Instead, knowing Theo wouldn't have asked about children if he didn't want forever with me, I felt nothing but joy and relief. That this man was mine for the rest of my life.

THE NEXT MORNING I WOKE UP TO FIND THE SPOT next to me in bed empty, the sheets still warm from Theo's body.

I grumbled, rubbing the sleep out of my eyes and squinting against the early morning light pouring in through the cracks in the curtains. "Where are you?" I called croakily.

"In the living room!"

"Why?" I muttered, grabbing my phone off the table and checking the time. Shit. It was nine o'clock in the morning. I kept forgetting it got lighter later in the day up here. "You're not writing already, are you?"

"Come see!"

I hissed at how cold the floorboards were beneath my feet and reminded myself to look into underfloor heating if we were going to be living here several months out of the year. Throwing on a robe, I stumbled sleepily into the living room, delighted to see Theo had switched on the gas fire.

"What are you..." I trailed off at the sight of him standing at our desks. On his desk was a tray with breakfast pastries and a pot of coffee. On my desk was my closed laptop... and a velvet ring box sitting on it.

I gaped at it, wondering if it was what I thought it was.

"Come here, little darling," he murmured, his words husky with emotion.

Slowly, I crossed the room to him, my gaze glued to the ring box on my laptop.

A touch at my chin brought my eyes to his. He'd bent his head, searching my face. There was anxiety in his expression. How could he possibly be anxious? Surely he knew by now he was my everything.

My lips parted with a small gasp of emotion as Theo slowly lowered himself to one knee in front of me. He gave me a strangely nervous smile that didn't suit him at all.

"I thought of a million ways to do this. Astonishing, grand

ways to ask you this. In the end, I went with what felt right."
He gestured to the desks. "This is where I fell in love with you.
Fell so fucking hard that your love broke me into pieces and
put me back together as a better man."

A sob whimpered between my lips, desperate to release,
but I didn't want to miss a single word.

Theo reached for the ring box and opened it before me.

I smothered a gasp with my palm, disbelieving the sight.
The engagement was clearly vintage and so perfect for me, I
could have cried. It was elegant and unassuming, the diamond
set on a platinum claw shaped like a flower bud. There was a
subtle carving on either side of the band.

"The last two years have been the best of my life," Theo
continued, eyes bright with emotion. "It's all because of you.
And I would be a fool to ever let you go, Sarah McCulloch. So
will you do me and the world a favor—because I would be a
bastard to deal with otherwise—the great honor of becoming
Mrs. Cavendish?"

Blood rushing in my ears, skin tingling and hot, I lowered
myself slowly to my knees so I could capture his handsome
face in my hands. "The honor would be all mine, Mr.
Cavendish. No one has ever loved me as well as you, and I
know no one ever will." My tears slipped free, rolling in warm
streaks down my cheeks. "And I promise no one could ever
love you as much as I do. Yes, I will marry you."

I'd barely gotten the last word out when Theo hauled me
into his arms to kiss me breathless. Somewhere in between the
kisses he scattered across my lips and face and neck, he slipped
the ring on my finger.

It fitted perfectly.

I crawled over him until he sat back on his arse, and I
straddled him. His arms banded tightly around me. The ring
glinted on my finger as I smoothed my hands over his face and
into his hair. We just gazed upon one another for the longest

time, just drinking in the momentous occasion and the hope of what the future held for us. I realized that this was why he'd brought up the subject of children yesterday. He'd wanted me to feel secure about our future no matter what, so I'd have no reservations about saying yes.

I kissed him, pouring every ounce of love into it. His fingers dug into my back and he grew hard between my legs. But it wasn't about sex right then. I knew because the heat that pooled low in my belly was inspired by our love more than anything else. I loved him so much I couldn't remember a time, or cared to remember a time, when I existed without this love inside me.

Pulling back, I brushed my lips over his, soothing him and the intensity of feeling I knew was bubbling through him. "Just so you know, this was the most perfect proposal. It was everything and more than I could ever want."

I didn't need grand, outlandish displays of affection.

I didn't want that.

I wanted simple honesty because it meant more.

This *was* where we'd fallen in love, writing Juno together. He couldn't have picked a more perfect place or more perfect words.

Theo rested his forehead between the crook of my neck and I felt all that tension from yesterday melt out of him. "I love you, Mrs. Cavendish," he whispered hoarsely.

Even though I wasn't Mrs. Cavendish legally, we both knew I was in our hearts. Tightening my embrace, I pressed my lips to his ear. "I love you, Mr. Cavendish."

ALLEGRA

As I walked through the door, my arm looped through my dad's, my heels clicking lightly on the wooden floors, I couldn't imagine a moment as far removed from the day I married Jared. The first time. Then it had just been the two of us and strangers to witness it.

"You happy?" Dad asked under his breath as we followed the aisle that was demarcated by rows of flowers and fairy lights on either side. The song Dandelions by Ruth B. accompanied my walk down the aisle. Every time I heard that song, it reminded me of Jared and how it felt like forever that I'd loved him, all the while wishing he'd love me back.

Set up in the village hall were rows of chairs decorated with blush bows for our guests to sit on. The village hall was home to ceilidhs and village celebrations. When we were deciding where to get married for the second time, the village hall seemed like the perfect choice. We both wanted it to feel quintessentially like home, and this building was an important part of Ardnoch.

To my mother's chagrin.

She'd wanted us to get married at the Balmoral Hotel in Edinburgh.

We'd wanted something smaller, quieter. Less elaborate. More meaningful. More us.

And there weren't rows upon rows of chairs either.

Just enough to seat our guests. My family, Jared's cousin Sarah and her husband Theo, and their baby daughter Rose (named after Theo's mother). Sloane, Walker, Callie and Harry. Georgie and his wife. Anna and hers. A few locals I considered friends, including Morag and Flora. The entire Adair family, who were growing exponentially and took up most of our guest list. Murmurings of restless kids filled the room, and I didn't mind a bit.

My eyes moved past the guests to where my husband stood at the altar. At the sight of him, so handsome in his kilt, my breathing stuttered. He'd gone for the full regalia, kilt, jacket, waistcoat, sporran, and the fly plaid of his family's personal tartan draped over one shoulder and fastened with an amber and silver brooch.

I didn't know what it was about a Scotsman in a kilt but it did it for me every time.

Jared was too busy staring at me as if I was an angel sent from heaven to notice the lust mingling with my love on my expression.

Though we'd kept the ceremony small, we'd went all out with the wedding decor and clothing to make up for the starkness of our first ceremony. My dress was the dress of my dreams. It was a fairy-tale and me to a T. The skirt of the gown was made of a pale blush tulle that flared out from a cinched in Chantilly lace bodice. The bodice was covered in frosted beading with petal appliqués that cascaded down the gown. It was strapless with a plunging sweetheart neckline that made the dress just a little sexy. I felt like a princess in it.

And Jared was looking at me with such awe, it made tears shimmer in my eyes.

"I've never been happier," I promised my dad.

I caught Aria's gaze. She was already waiting at the altar as my maid of honor, Callie and Sloane at her side as my bridesmaids. They all wore blush pink dresses, but I'd let them choose the style. My big sister usually suited jewel tones better, but she looked gorgeous and classy in a blush-colored pencil dress. Joy for me brimmed over in her eyes.

To everyone's surprise, Jared had chosen Theo to be his best man. Sarah's husband stood at my husband's side with baby Rose in his arms. If he was possessive of Sarah, he was even more so over his daughter. I smiled at the sight of the unlikely father and child, before Jared pulled my attention back to him just by existing.

As we reached the end of the aisle, Dad turned me to him, his gaze searching my face. "I am so proud of you," he whispered hoarsely. He'd been extremely emotional this past year, as if a dam had broken inside of him when all the truth came tumbling out.

He and Mom had taken a break for a while. But they'd recently gotten back together and were trying to make it work. They'd both agreed to couple's therapy, and I hoped it worked out for them. I truly did. But whatever happened, I'd be there for them both. I wanted a fresh start in life, not just with Jared, but with all the people I loved.

"Thanks, Dad." I kissed his cheek, and he took my hand and led me to my husband.

Jared slid his fingers through mine and pulled me to him.

Laughter caught in my breath at his eagerness.

"You look so fucking beautiful," he whispered hoarsely, his gaze devouring. "I can't believe you're mine."

"You too." I leaned into him, and he rested his forehead against mine.

The collective sigh in the room reminded us we had an audience.

A throat clearing brought our heads up, and we turned to find North grinning knowingly at us.

When deciding who would officiate, I knew I'd wanted it to be someone who knew us. My brother-in-law was a born entertainer... but more than that, he'd witnessed our journey and he cared about us. We were already legally married. My visa application had come through. This ceremony was just our way of letting the world and each other know that we truly were in love. So North could officiate with no need to be ordained.

He made a gesture to someone at the back of the room and the song Dandelions faded out.

"Distinguished guests," North's powerful voice boomed around the hall, "We're gathered here today to witness this man and this woman unite, *again*, in holy matrimony."

Our guests tittered at his pointed 'again' while I gave my brother-in-law a droll look.

North's answering smile was affectionate. "I, for one, feel honored to be here."

'Love you', I mouthed.

He gave me a nod as if to say 'you too.' "Allegra, you are more than a sister in name to me and I couldn't be prouder of the extraordinary woman you've become. I'm relieved and grateful that the man you've chosen as yours comes closer than most to deserving you."

Soft laughter filled our ears as Jared's grin flashed, and he nodded in agreement.

"So... without further ado..." North gave me a slight bow of his head. "Allegra Emma Howard McCulloch, do you retake Jared McCulloch to be your lawfully wedded husband?"

I turned, looking deep into Jared's eyes. "I do. And for the record, you deserve me. We deserve each other."

Jared's lips tugged up at the corner.

"That's a matter of opinion, but we'll continue," North cracked and Jared just shook his head, taking my brother-in-law's ribbing in good spirit. "Jared McCulloch, do you retake Allegra Emma Howard McCulloch to be your lawfully wedded wife?"

"I do," Jared's voice was hoarse with feeling as his gaze moved over my face like he was imprinting the image of me on his brain forever.

"You can take this moment to say your vows. Make it good, Jared."

Laughter bubbled on my lips as my husband cut North a filthy look before turning back to me. His expression melted into a smolder that came naturally, and made me want to rip his kilt right off.

"I hope in our time as a married couple," Jared began, "I've made it clear to you how much I love you. But if I haven't, I need you to know that before you my life was just a matter of going through the motions. I got up every morning and I worked a farm I love. But there was nothing to truly look forward to until you."

An ache pierced across my chest. A fantastic kind of ache.

"Every morning I wake up... and I wake up for you. I wake up looking forward to life because you're in mine. You are every second, every minute, and every hour of my day, every day. And you will be for the rest of my life."

Tears threatened to ruin my mascara. My husband had a habit of surprising me with the most perfect words.

"I love you, Allegra McCulloch. I vow to never stop loving you because it's a vow I know I'll never break."

I swallowed hard around the thickness in my throat and squeezed his hands.

"Well," North stared at Jared like he'd never seen him before... then he looked at me. "I dare you top that."

I rolled my eyes as more laughter filled my ears. "I can't!" I complained half-heartedly. "He always says the perfect thing. Always." I leaned toward Jared. "I love you. It's as simple as that. You make me feel seen. You always have. For so long, I was just drifting. Until Ardnoch. And I know now that the reason I clung onto this place is that part of me knew, even before we fell in love, that this was the place where the other half of me existed. That other half was with you. And for as long as I live, it will always be with you. I'm not whole without you, Jared." A tear slipped free. "I never will be. You are the most honorable, kind, loyal, sexy man I've ever met. I love you so much."

Jared's eyes gleamed with emotion and need.

"Beautiful." North's eyes gleamed. "Okay then. Well...by the power invested in me by no one," he teased, "I now pronounce you husband and wife. For real this time because nobody bought that half-arsed lie the first time around."

Our guests burst into shocked laughter as I gaped at North, unsure whether to laugh or smack him. But the sound of Jared's chuckle made my decision for me. I turned from glowering in horror at North to find Jared smiling that sexy smile of his. Then before anyone could say another word, he slid his arms around my waist, crushed his mouth over mine and dipped me in a flare of uncharacteristic dramatics.

I giggled against his kiss, clinging to his lapels as the sound of wolf whistles and clapping filled my ears.

It was perfect.

Our wedding was perfect.

Simple, but full of love.

It was everything Jared and I could ever want or need.

CALLIE

The joyful combined noise of the fiddle, accordion, guitar, bodhran drum, and flute filled the village hall as our family, friends, and neighbors danced with abandonment. Lewis's face was lit with laughter and happiness as he spun me out and pulled me back against his body. My laughter joined the ruckus as he did it again, making me slightly dizzy.

Only a few hours earlier I'd walked down the aisle in an off-white gown with bat-wing lace sleeves and a deep V back with flowers and lace applique in the floor-length skirt. The gown had a sneaky, sexy split, so I flashed a leg as I walked. A wreath of flowers sat around my head and I wore flat sandals with flowers attached to the straps. Everything about my wedding gown screamed boho princess. And I matched Lewis perfectly in his kilt (in Adair tartan colors, of course) that he'd paired with chunky, well-worn biker boots.

We'd gotten married across the street at Ardnoch church and my husband-to-be waited for me at the altar with our beautiful baby girl in his arms. Harley had stayed in Lewis's embrace the entire ceremony (sleeping through most of it, like the angel baby she was) because we couldn't imagine not including our daughter in our union.

An hour ago, my new aunt and uncle by marriage had taken Harley home with them for the night. It was my first night without her and Lewis had to drag me back into the village hall after I'd taken twenty minutes to say goodbye to her. Arro and Mac had assured me she'd be fine. I was so grateful to them for volunteering to be the ones to cut out of the wedding early to babysit her. Their daughter, Skye, was happy to leave with her parents and even more excited to have Harley with them.

Lewis had set upon taking me around all our guests to thank them as a distraction tactic. I knew I needed to suck it up and get over my attachment issues because Lewis and I were departing on our honeymoon tomorrow. We weren't going far because I drew the line at being in a different country from Harley, so we were taking his Harley Davidson on a road trip to a luxury cabin Lewis had booked us south of Inverness. That's all I knew. The rest was a mystery.

Lewis pulled me close, his lips brushing my ear. "Happy?"

I nodded, smiling, because honestly I felt like I might burst with all the bliss.

I was finally Mrs. Callie Adair.

My husband banded his arms around me, pressing a hard kiss to my temple as we swayed out of beat with the joyous music. My gaze went over his shoulder as we held each other close and landed on Eilidh, who was showing her wee sister Morwenna how to ceilidh dance. Mor's giggles made me smile harder. The teen seemed to glow under her big sister's attention. Eilidh wrapped an arm around Mor's shoulders and they danced together. It had been ages since I'd seen Eils look so free and happy. She was literally here for a day and then had to travel back to London first thing in the morning to film the popular British dramedy she starred in.

My gaze drifted past her to Fyfe. He'd stood at Lewis's side as best man and was handsome in the kilt that matched my husband's. He'd also come solo to the wedding. I watched him throw back an impressive gulp of whisky, his lips quirking as he watched Eilidh with Mor.

I stiffened a little as I recognized the look on his face as he stared at Eilidh.

It was a hungry look Lewis gave me almost daily.

"What is it?" My husband asked, pulling away to look at me.

"Nothing," I lied quickly.

He narrowed his eyes.

"Just missing Harley." I shrugged sheepishly. It wasn't a fib.

He cupped my face in his hands. "I know. But we'll see her before we leave tomorrow, and if it's too much, we can always come home."

I nodded.

Since the moment we'd brought Harley home from the hospital, it was as if a piece I'd been missing my whole life suddenly clicked into place. Aye, we were exhausted all the time, especially in the first few months, and it was a level of exhaustion I had no idea humans were capable of without losing all ability to function. But the love we felt for her was worth everything. Then a few months ago, a miracle occurred. Harley started sleeping. So much so I was worried enough to take her to the doctor. Dr. Mulligan just smiled and reassured me that some babies slept better than others. It didn't seem to be a fluke, either. Harley was nine months old, and she'd been sleeping through the night for three months straight.

For the first six weeks I still got up to check on her, much to Lewis's amusement, but I'd finally relaxed into sleeping through the night too.

I didn't know how much longer our luck would hold out,

but both of us were feeling fairly human again now that we were sleeping. She even slept during the day when she was supposed to. In fact, Harley seemed to adore sleeping. Which made me wonder if we'd pay for our good luck when she was old enough to go to school and we had to haul her out of bed.

After the ceilidh band finished their set, the DJ we'd hired played an eclectic mix of songs, but not so loud people couldn't have a conversation. Then Dad claimed me for the father-daughter dance and I felt my eyes burn with tears before he even led me out to the dance floor. Dad noted my unshed tears and I saw the tender amusement in his eyes. I caught Mum's gaze, and that just made me want to bawl even more. She'd been emotional the entire day.

I'd gone back and forth about who would walk me down the aisle. Mum had been both mother and father to me for the first ten years of my life, my protector and safe haven. But Walker Ironside had taken on the role of my dad as if he was born to it. No questions asked. He'd loved me like I was his own from the moment he entered my life.

In the end, I'd asked them both to walk me down the aisle and give me away.

"Will you look after Mum tonight?" I asked Dad as he held me in his arms. I could feel everyone watching us, but I shut them out as I stared up into his rugged, handsome face.

"When have I ever not?" he assured me.

Very true. "I know. I just... I think the wedding is hitting her harder than me moving in with Lewis." I hoped she didn't think she was losing me somehow. That would never happen. And not just because we ran a business together.

"It's not what you think." Dad squeezed my hand. "Your mum is relieved."

"Relieved?"

He nodded. "It took her going through some serious shit to end up in a place she was safe and happy. When you and

Lewis split as kids, she was worried. She wanted nothing but smooth sailing for you, kid."

Of course she did. I smiled. "That's not realistic."

"No. But it's what you want for Harley, right?"

"Absolutely."

"Seeing you so happy with Harley, with Lewis, and you're only twenty-six... aye, your mum's relieved. Relieved you found everything you need so soon so you can just enjoy the rest of your life."

His words made me feel so much better. I hated the idea of my mum feeling lost or sad about me becoming an Adair. I searched Dad's face as he stared back at me, stoic to the outside world. But I knew Walker Ironside. He was a big softie underneath that intimidating façade. "I've had a lot of good things happen to me. Harley, Lewis. The first good thing that happened to me was being born Mum's kid. The second was the day you adopted me."

The muscle in his jaw twitched as his grip on me tightened.

"I couldn't have asked for a better dad. Thank you for being mine."

He swallowed hard, visibly fighting back the emotion as he pulled me to him to press a kiss to my temple. "Couldn't have given you away to anyone less deserving than Adair."

I smiled, tears trembling on my lashes. "I know. And even though I'm technically now an Adair... I hope you know that I'll always be an Ironside."

"Quit it, kid, before I lose my shit in front of all these people," he grumbled.

I grinned harder, watching as Lewis approached his mum, Regan, to ask her to dance.

Soon the dancefloor was filled again. Regan and Dad danced with one another as Lewis danced with Mum, and I danced with my new father-in-law, Thane.

By the end of the night, most of us were absolutely smashed on the Ardnoch whisky our uncles had donated to the wedding reception. I barely remembered which sober friend drove me and Lewis home, but I remembered waking up with a pounding headache in the morning and a little regret that we'd both passed out on our wedding night. Still, it had been a bloody amazing reception.

HARLEY CRAWLED ON THE FLOOR OF MUM AND Dad's living room, her wee giggles like pops of sunshine. My chest ached and I bent down and swooped her into my arms. Settling her on my hips, I spoke nonsense to her as she clapped her hands and giggled harder.

To my utter delight, I'd gotten my wish and Harley had Lewis's blue eye color. All the baby books I'd read told me that at nine months her true eye color should be evident, so I was relieved they wouldn't lighten to my shade of blue.

Harley had incredibly long eyelashes for a baby, and I didn't think I was biased when I said she was utterly beautiful. Beneath the massive bow headband Regan had put on Harley this morning was already a good head of dark hair. Just like Lewis. Her plump, warm, delicious weight in my arms was my favorite feeling in the world, and I couldn't believe I wouldn't see her for five nights.

"Are you going to be good for gran and grandpa?" I asked her.

She made a meh sound that made Mum (gran) laugh.

"And nana and papa will come see you lots too I'm sure." Nana and papa being Regan and Thane. Tears filled my eyes as I cuddled her against me and pressed a long kiss to her forehead.

"It's okay." Lewis soothed a hand over my back. "It's just

five nights and she's got a million people who love her looking after her."

"I know." I whimpered before pressing another kiss or ten to her face and cheeks.

She squirmed impatiently in my arms, stretching out a chubby hand to Lewis. I handed her over to her dad so he could say goodbye. That feeling in my chest grew so big, like always, as I watched Lewis with our daughter. She was so tiny in his arms as he bounced her, making her laugh. Then I saw the flash of uncertainty on his face too as he kissed her cheek and cuddled her against his neck.

"She'll be fine," I reassured him now.

"Okay, time to intervene." Mum crossed the room and gently removed Harley from Lewis's arms. She smiled at us. "Off you go before you decide not to. Enjoy your honeymoon. We'll enjoy some quality time with our granddaughter."

SINCE WE WERE ONLY GOING FOR FIVE NIGHTS AND we had no plans but to be in the cabin and with nature for those five nights, all of our luggage fit into the smallish luggage box Lewis bought for his motorbike. The cabin Lewis had booked was only an hour and twenty minutes south of Ardnoch by car. On the Harley, it was almost half that.

Still, I enjoyed every second on the back of the bike as we rode like the wind. The ride helped relax me and did its best to dissuade the mum guilt I was currently experiencing.

There was no need to stop for a break and soon we were driving off the A831 and down a road that twisted through the tall pines we'd rode by. The drive down past the majestic mountains had been extraordinary and was over way too fast. Now Lewis was riding up, up through the winding forest of pines until a clearing opened up on the rise of the hill. He slowed to a stop outside a large log cabin. A neighboring cabin was across the way.

We pulled off our helmets and I turned back to look at the stunning view down toward the valley of the mountains.

As we got off the bike, stretching our legs, I grinned at Lewis, letting some of my excitement at being in this beautiful place with my husband, alone, for five nights creep in. The log cabin we'd parked outside of was the reception, where a man maybe ten years older than us who introduced himself as Andrew greeted us. He provided information on the local tourist things to do, a map of all the walks on the property, and directions on how to get to our cabin.

This time, Lewis took the trail slowly as we looked for our cabin. We kept winding up and up until finally we found it perked right on the top of a steep face.

Holy hell... the view.

"Lewis," I whispered in awe as he took my hand and led me into the log cabin.

It was stunning. Beautifully appointed with open plan living and a mezzanine level bedroom. French doors led out onto the wrap around deck, and the deck perched out over the expansive, stunning view of rugged green and brown and amber mountains plunging down toward the green-blue surface of an inland loch. We were so high up, mist coated the edges of the loch and trees. It was magical.

Crisp, fresh air filled our lungs as we took it all in.

"We're in paradise for five days."

Lewis pulled me back against his chest. "Aye, we are."

Inside the log cabin, we discovered the bed covered in rose petals and there was a bottle of expensive champagne in an ice bucket, along with some local baked goods and chocolates. A card from the owners wished us a happy honeymoon.

"What do you want to do?" I asked Lewis as we stood downstairs. "Hike, go for a walk, ride?"

In answer, Lewis shrugged off his jacket, his gaze suddenly smoldering.

"Oh." Tingles of anticipation exploded between my thighs.

He then yanked off his T-shirt. "I want to make love to my wife."

Arousal flushed through me as I shed my jacket and top. "Good plan, Husband."

Lewis grinned. "This is the first time in nine months that you can be really, really fucking loud."

"Then you better give me reason to be loud, Mr. Adair."

"Oh intend to, Mrs. Adair." He prowled toward me, unzipping his jeans. "I intend to."

***

My cries of pleasure filled the cabin as Lewis powered into me from behind. He had me bent over the kitchen table, my nipples grazing against the wood, my fingernails digging into the surface as he fucked me like there was no tomorrow.

Our first night at the cabin had been a leisurely, lovely, languid night of lovemaking.

The second day we'd gone for long walks, had a picnic, and then spent the evening fucking.

The third day, we went on a boat ride, had a pub lunch, had sex when we got home and then watched a couple of movies.

The fourth day we'd stayed in the cabin all day, lazing in bed, talking between bouts of energetic lovemaking.

Our last night in the cabin, Lewis seemed to realize it was our last night and was utterly insatiable. I was not complaining.

He gripped my hip in one strong hand, while the other

pressed down on my back, keeping me in place. I could do nothing but take his fucking, and it was utterly stupendous.

When I came, lights exploded behind my eyes and I lost myself for a minute as my inner muscles clamped around Lewis's cock in hard, throbbing waves.

My husband's guttural groan of pleasure filled the cabin as my release hurried along his climax.

"Oh fuck, oh fuck, oh fuck," he panted as his hips shuddered against my arse.

I was pretty sure I'd melded with the kitchen table.

Even as Lewis finally got himself together enough to pull out, I couldn't move. I heard him practically growl as I felt his cum drip between my thighs. His hand smoothed over my arse. "I'll want you again soon," he warned me.

I grunted in response, my whole body like jelly.

"Are you alive?" he asked, amused.

I grunted again.

He laughed softly before I felt his hands on me. Lewis easily lifted me off the table and into his arms, bridal style. I cuddled into him as he carried me into the bathroom and set me down on the edge of the bath. The large bathtub sat at a vast window that overlooked the mountains. Not very private, but unless someone was out there in a helicopter, no one was going to see you naked in the tub. I watched him as he ran the water and filled it with a citrusy smelling bubble bath.

When it was ready, I slipped in and he got in behind me, my back against his chest.

As we lazed together, sexually replete, staring out at the impressive view, I took a mental snapshot.

I'd missed Harley terribly since we'd left, but I'd realized something while I enjoyed alone time with Lewis. I'd missed him, too. I'd missed having his uninterrupted attention and giving him mine. I'd missed being able to cry and pant and scream his name as he pleasured my body and I his.

And I'd decided I would not wish those moments away. Now that we were parents, we wouldn't have this all the time. These moments together wouldn't be a daily occurrence. Or even a weekly or monthly one. If we were lucky, we could steal that time on rare occasions or once a year on a long weekend away together.

"I miss Harley and can't wait to see her... but I'm going to miss this, too." I trailed my fingers down his brawny, tattooed forearm.

"You don't need to miss this, Mo Chridhe." He kissed my cheek. "Anytime you want me like this, one of our parents will be happy to take Harley for the night."

"We could do that?"

"As long as we're not abusing their kindness, aye. Maybe we should even make it a thing. Instead of date night once a month, we do fuck night."

I snort laughed. "I think my lack of romanticism is rubbing off on you."

His chest shook against my back as he chuckled. "I'd just forgotten how much of a turn on it is when you're loud. When we can both be loud."

I felt his cock twitch behind my back.

So I turned in his arms, water splashing everywhere. Lewis adjusted his legs so I could straddle him. Reaching beneath the water for him, I gripped him in my hand and caressed him until he was hard and throbbing. The whole time I held his gaze. Then I planted my hands on his shoulders, he grasped my waist and I pushed down on him. I gasped, arching my back as he eased inside me.

"Fuck, Callie." Lewis cupped my breasts, his thumbs brushing over my nipples as I gently rode him. The water continued to splash everywhere, but I didn't care. I rode him slowly, feeling powerful and sexy under his hungry gaze.

"Sometimes I can't believe you're mine. My wife," he panted, squeezing my breasts as pleasure suffused his face.

I tightened my inner muscles around him and Lewis groaned.

"Are you close?"

"So close." He gripped my waist now. "You have to come, baby."

"Tell me what you're going to do to me when we get out of the tub?"

His eyes flared. He knew his dirty talking was a surefire way to get me off. "I'm going to spread you out on that kitchen table again and eat your sweet pussy."

"Oh, yes, yes." My pace increased. "More."

He slapped my arse, hard, and I shuddered. "Lewis!"

"I'm going to tie you to the bed and you're going to take my big cock in that tight pussy and I'll take you how I want. And you'll take it, mo chridhe. You'll take it how I like to give it. Hard and dirty. Because your pussy belongs to me."

"Yes, yes!"

His hand cracked over my arse again. "Come around my cock, baby. Let me feel your wet."

That was it. I shattered around him with a cry of his name and felt him throb with release inside of me.

We kissed as we shuddered together through our release.

When we finally broke free, I pressed my face to his throat and whispered, "We're definitely doing a monthly fuck night."

His arms tightened around me as he laughed.

As SAD AS I WAS TO LEAVE BEHIND THE CABIN, LEWIS promised we'd be back, and I had holding my baby girl in my arms to look forward to.

Harley had burst into tears as soon as we walked into my

parent's house, adding to my mum-guilt. However, by the time we brought her home to our 'wee castle' in the woods, she was her bright, cheery self again. As I cooked in the kitchen, Lewis played with Harley in the sitting room. His deep, soft laughter mingled with her high-pitched squeals and I wanted to burst into sobbing tears.

Happy, messy, sobbing tears.

I knew life wouldn't always be this sweet. That we'd hit hard times. We'd face loss. That was life. But it was these sweet moments, feeling like I had everything in the world anyone could ever dream of having, that would get me through the bad times.

My mum had always been my safe haven. She always would be.

But I had another one now. Harley and Lewis and any future children who came along would fill this house with so much love I'd never feel anything but safe in it.

I would never take for granted how lucky I was to have two safe havens to return home to.

Eilidh

"Are you enjoying staying with Granny Regan?" I asked Millie via video call on my phone. Fyfe stood behind me, arms casually wrapped around my waist, his chin on my shoulder.

Millie stood between my mother's thighs, resting her back against Mum's chest as Mum kneeled. Our daughter's dark blue eyes had lightened in the last few years and with her dark hair (currently tied into two high adorable pigtails), people often remarked that she could be my biological daughter. Millie's lips pursed before she responded, "Aye." But she leaned into the phone, trying to grab it from my mother's hand. "Mummy, when you comin' home?"

An ache scored across my chest, and Fyfe's embrace tightened. "Just a wee bit longer, my love."

Frowning with all the beleaguered impatience of a forty-year-old at my vague response, her gaze moved to Fyfe. "Daddy, when you comin' home?"

I felt the vibration of his amusement as he tried to stifle his laughter. "One more week, wee yin. That'll fly in. Especially because Granny Regan has lots of fun things planned."

Millie tilted her head to look up at Mum. "Aye?"

Mum smiled, affectionately smoothing back the loose strands of Millie's hair with her free hand. "Zoo tomorrow. We're going on a road trip to see the tigers." Mills was obsessed with tigers.

Her sweet face lit up. "Tigers?"

Mum grinned. "And lots of other cool animals."

Millie's head whipped back to me. "Are you comin' with us?"

Ugh, this killed me.

I didn't realize being away from her would be so difficult.

The tears brightening my eyes reminded me there was something else at play that made me so emotional about our temporary separation.

Fyfe, sensing my fight to not cry in front of our toddler, explained, "It's just a fun trip for you and Granny Regan."

"And you," she insisted stubbornly, jutting out her chin.

"Not this time, wee yin."

"Why?"

"Because we're on a special mummy and daddy trip."

"Why?"

Fyfe cleared the laughter from his throat. Millie's favorite word right now was 'why?'. "Because Mummy and Daddy got married this year and our trip is to celebrate that."

Technically, we were married two months ago. But our schedules hadn't aligned until now. It was a late honeymoon.

"Why?"

Mum laughed. "We could be here all day with the whys. Say bye bye to Mum and Dad."

"We'll check in to see how the zoo trip goes," I hurried to say. "Bye bye, my love. Have an amazing time with the tigers."

"Bye, wee yin. Love you."

A mulish expression clouded our daughter's face and I knew if she didn't say goodbye, I'd start sobbing.

"Say bye, Millie." Mum waved at us. "You'll see Mum and Dad soon."

Thankfully, Millie waved. "Bye."

Mum switched off the video before I could draw out the torture. "Well, that was rude," I huffed.

Fyfe chuckled as I turned in his arms. "If your mum didn't do that, Millie would have just gotten upset again."

"Don't remind me." I pulled from his embrace, sniffling as I tried to hold back tears.

"Eilidh."

I glanced back at him.

We stood in a luxurious hotel suite in a five-star hotel on the banks of Lake Como in Italy. When Fyfe asked where I wanted to spend our honeymoon, I'd chosen the destination based on food. We'd been in Como for three nights already and planned to leave for Venice in the morning for another few days before traveling onto Bologna for the last leg of the trip. It was our first holiday alone together.

My husband tried not to look disappointed and failed. "Our daughter is safe and happy. We're alone for the first time since we got together... and you're miserable."

Remorse filled me. "No." I crossed the room, looping my arms around his neck, pressing my body against his. "I'm not miserable. I love being alone with you."

Fyfe's hands rested on my hips, and he squeezed. "Something is going on. If... if you want to go home... if it's too soon for you to be away from Millie, then we can go home early."

Love. Immeasurable love flooded through my veins for this man. I'd been an emotional wreck for the last few weeks. Crying over the least wee thing. Fyfe assumed it was nervousness about leaving Millie and had hoped it would dissipate with time.

It wasn't the reason at all. Okay, it was a little the reason. I'd started the process of legally adopting Millie a year ago. Her biological mother, Pamela, willingly gave up her rights. Millie's adoption papers came through just after the wedding. I already loved Millie like she was mine, but to have it be official was the best wedding gift anyone could give me.

And perhaps that's why I was such a jumble of mixed emotions right now.

Seeing Fyfe's concerned (and somewhat glum) expression, I realized I couldn't wait until the end of our honeymoon to tell him my news like I'd planned. Previously, I'd planned to tell him in Bologna on our last night.

However, I couldn't leave him thinking for the rest of the week that I didn't want to be on our honeymoon.

"Fyfe..." Taking hold of his hand, I guided it from my hip along my still flat stomach. "I'm eight weeks pregnant."

His lips parted, and a little whoosh of air released from him.

We hadn't planned to get pregnant just yet. We'd discussed waiting another year. But the universe had other plans and apparently Fyfe's swimmers were stronger than birth control.

Swallowing hard, Fyfe's gaze dropped to my belly as his hand moved over it. "You're pregnant?"

"Yes."

"We're having a baby?"

"Yes. And my hormones are all over the place. I'm so excited and nervous and terrified and overjoyed and scared that our relationship will change because we'll have two small children to look after and worried that Millie will think she's being replaced." There. I blurted out all my concerns. Everything I'd bottled up since I found out I was pregnant three weeks ago.

Fyfe tenderly cupped my face. "Millie was dropped on us like the world's best surprise and we rose to the occasion. We took care of her and loved her and we did it all the while untangling our feelings for one another. We started our relationship as parents to a not even one-year-old baby. Having another, and this time getting to go through the entire pregnancy together, to be there from day one... it's going to be magical, Eilidh. I'm going to love every second because I know what it's like to be deprived of that privilege."

Tears burned my eyes. "Fyfe..."

"And Millie could never think she's being replaced. You love her too much."

"I thought that, though," I whispered. "When Mum fell pregnant with Mor... I worried she'd love her more than me."

"She doesn't. She loves you both. And you know that's how you'll be, Eilidh. Even if Millie ever has those thoughts as she grows up, you can relate to her, and she'll believe you more than anyone: that love just doesn't work like that."

"I love you so much." Tears rolled down my cheeks before I could stop them.

My husband did a valiant job of attempting to kiss every single one away. He embraced me. "I love you more than I thought I could love anyone," he responded gruffly. "Wife. Mother of my children."

I grinned, pulling back to look him in the eyes. "Do you want to stay in the room today?"

Heat darkened his gaze. "What did you have in mind?"

I tugged him toward the bed. "As well as being very teary with the hormones... I'm also feeling very needy."

"Needy?" Fyfe grinned, gently easing me down on the bed.

"Extremely. I have an ever-growing list of things I'd like you to do to me while we're free to be as loud as we want."

"Tell me of this list," his voice was hoarse with want before he brushed his lips across my throat. "In vivid detail."

Shivers cascaded around my breasts and my lower belly clenched with anticipation. "Well... it all starts with a little role playing."

His head came up, his eyebrow raised with intrigue. "Go on."

"In this scenario...I'm playing the forbidden little sister of your best friend."

Fyfe's lips twitched as he caressed my breast. "Is that right?"

"Mmm." I arched into his touch. "Totally off-limits. But one day, we're left all alone in my bedroom..."

"And I just can't help myself," he continues, his hand sliding down my hip to between my legs, "Because all I can think about is your smile, your lips, the way you look at me... You make me so hard. And one day—"

"We're laughing and joking, play wrestling over something stupid," my breath hitches as his hand dips beneath my shorts and underwear, "And you—"

"Feel your sweet tits pressed to my body and lose my mind. I have to touch you, have to feel you." His fingers find my clit and I gasp. "You're so wet." Fyfe watches me as my pleasure intensifies with his massage. "I forget I'm not supposed to have you. All I can think about is thrusting my cock into your tight wee pussy and coming inside you. Bare," he growls. "Fuck, I want to see my cum all over you."

"Yes, yes," I gasp as my climax nears.

"Before we know it, I'm pulling your knickers down and thrusting into you. Fucking you on your bedroom floor. You love every second."

"Yes, yes!"

"I tear at your shirt, need to see your tits." He does just that with his free hand and I almost tip over the edge. "They're perfect. Your nipples. I want them in my mouth. I fuck you harder. So hard. You cry out my name. I'm begging you to come around me. Anyone could hear us but we don't care. And then you come, your tight, hot cunt squeezing around my cock until I see heaven."

My climax hit and as I cried out, the tension inside me shattering, I was vaguely aware of my husband divesting me of my shorts and underwear before he shrugged off his own.

He was hard and throbbing as he moved over me, guiding his cock between my thighs.

"Realization dawns." His words are gruff. "I've just fucked my best friend's little sister."

I smile, delighted he was still playing out my fantasy. "What do you do?"

"Well, I'm a horny young bloke with amazing stamina." He smiled cockily. "So I fuck you again." Pleasure suffused his face as he pressed inside me. "And realize it wasn't a dream. You really do feel like heaven. And I don't care about consequences. I don't care as long as I get to spend the rest of my life with you."

"Fyfe," I moaned his name as he pumped into me in slow, determined drives. "I love you."

"I love you more," he promised on a growl, eagerly watching my expression slacken with desire as the thick drag of him in and out pushed me toward orgasm again. "Mine. My wife."

"My husband." I slid my arms around his back, my nails scratching lightly over his skin. "Father of my baby."

His eyes flashed with intense need, and his drives increased. "Eilidh. My Eilidh."

"Yours," I agreed with a gasp of pleasure, arching my hips into his thrusts.

"Mine. Yours." He groaned. "Come. Come around my cock. Come hard. I need it. I need you."

"I'm close," I promised.

He slipped his hand between us, his thumb finding my clit. "Now. Come now, Eilidh."

Perhaps it was his touch or perhaps it was the demanding purr in his voice, but I shattered. My inner muscles tugged voluptuously around him and Fyfe's hips stuttered as he cursed, gritting his teeth seconds before I felt him throb with release. He groaned loudly, long and hard, still pumping into me as if trying to prolong his climax.

He shuddered over me, his lips against my throat as I smoothed a soothing hand over his back.

Eventually he pushed up, eyes holding mine for a second before he looked between us as he pulled out. He grunted, eyes flaring at the sight of his cum, and then shot me a wicked smile. "I hope you know we're definitely not leaving this room today."

"You know I'm good for it."

Fyfe gently eased me to my feet. "Let's take a bath."

"Mmm, that sounds nice." I had a fantasy or two about what we could do in a bathtub.

Pulling me into his arms, his hand drifted down to my belly again. "We're pregnant," he whispered.

"We are."

"How did I get this lucky, Eilidh Moray?"

My chest ached at his question. "By being you. My beautiful husband."

His smile was a little shy, which made it even sexier. "Happy Honeymoon, Mrs. Moray."

"Happy forever together, Mr. Moray."

About the Author

Samantha is a *New York Times*, *USA Today*, and *Wall Street Journal* bestselling author and a Goodreads Choice Awards Nominee. Samantha has written over 60 books and is published in 31 countries. She writes emotional and angsty romance, often set where she resides—in her beloved home country Scotland. Samantha splits her time between her family, writing and chasing after two very mischievous cavapoos.